**'You've been i** ~~ried woman for~~

A faint smile touche... I have,' he said quietly.

'Oh, how sad!' Ellen responded with genuine sorrow. 'What are you going to do?' For several seconds he locked eyes with her, as if making up his mind. 'Addan,' she suggested unhappily, 'leave her! There'll be another woman ——'

'No!' he said with finality, despair in the melting darkness of his glowing eyes.

**Dear Reader**

*Bemvido a Madeira*! Welcome to Madeira, our island for this month. You're most likely to have heard of it because of its famous wines, but there's far more to it than that — this flower-covered island, with its tranquil, charming atmosphere and dramatic scenery, is known as 'Lovers' Isle'. . . What better setting could there possibly be for Sara Wood's passionate romance? *Tenha uma boa viagem* — have a good journey!

*The Editor*

**The author says:**

'Take an island, spend 500 years doggedly hacking 2,000 miles of water channels out of solid rock. Laboriously terrace it by hand from sea to sky and fill it with sub-tropical plants. Result: Madeira! Identifying so many exotic flowers and trees defeated me, plantaholic though I am, but I squashed my fear of heights and braved some spectacular *levada* walks in the mountains. My reward? Sheer terror! Excitement, too, a sense of peace and scenery out of this world.'

*Sara Wood*

★ TURN TO THE BACK PAGES OF THIS BOOK FOR *WELCOME TO EUROPE*. . .OUR FASCINATING FACT-FILE ★

# THE DARK EDGE OF LOVE

BY

## SARA WOOD

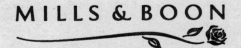

## MILLS & BOON

### MILLS & BOON LIMITED
ETON HOUSE, 18–24 PARADISE ROAD
RICHMOND, SURREY, TW9 1SR

*All the characters in this book have no existence outside the imagination of the Author, and have no relation whatsoever to anyone bearing the same name or names. They are not even distantly inspired by any individual known or unknown to the Author, and all the incidents are pure invention.*

*All Rights Reserved. The text of this publication or any part thereof may not be reproduced or transmitted in any form or by any means, electronic or mechanical, including photocopying, recording, storage in an information retrieval system, or otherwise, without the written permission of the publisher.*

*This book is sold subject to the condition that it shall not, by way of trade or otherwise, be lent, resold, hired out or otherwise circulated without the prior consent of the publisher in any form of binding or cover other than that in which it is published and without a similar condition including this condition being imposed on the subsequent purchaser.*

*First published in Great Britain 1994*
*by Mills & Boon Limited*

© *Sara Wood 1994*

*Australian copyright 1994*
*Philippine copyright 1994*
*This edition 1994*

ISBN 0 263 78422 3

*Set in 10 on 10½ pt Linotron Times*
*01-9403-58443*

*Typeset in Great Britain by Centracet, Cambridge*
*Made and printed in Great Britain*

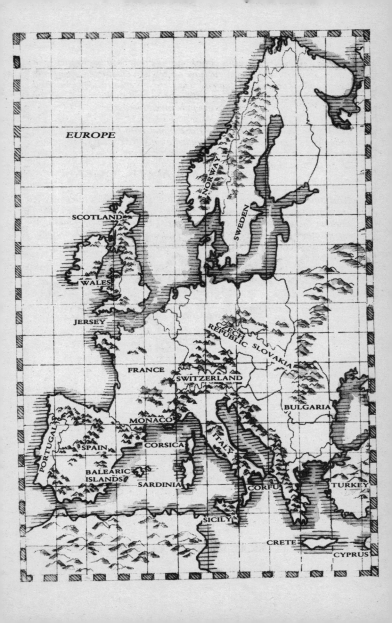

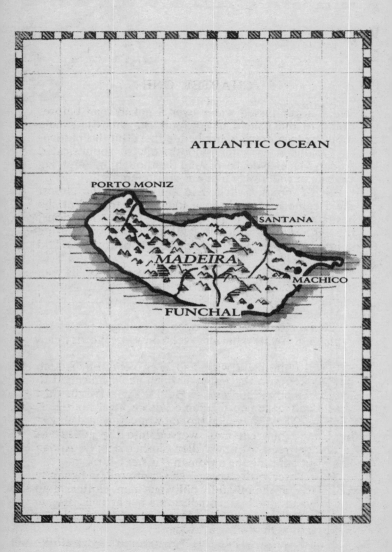

# CHAPTER ONE

SHE'D never tossed water over a naked man before. Come to that, she'd never found an uninvited male sprawled face-down in her bed, either! But this particular Goldilocks was the smooth, oh, so sophisticated Addan Machico de Torre, and the thought of emptying a carafe of water over him was *very* tempting.

Ellen's mouth twitched in amusement, the closest she'd come to a smile in a long, long time. Yet she hesitated. It wasn't in her nature to be malicious, though her vile brother-in-law richly deserved putting in his place. What was he doing here? She frowned. Did he. . .*know*?

Addan shifted, gave a sexy little wriggle of his lean hips, and she froze. From his drowsy mouth came a muffled, sleepy mumble. 'Maria. . .*faz favor*. . .'

Maria. Please.

Ellen's mouth dropped open in outrage, a mystery explained. 'Well! What a nerve! You——!' Words failed her.

It was quite clear what had been going on. Addan had broken into the house—which she'd imagined to have been empty for a year. He'd dragged off the dust sheets and begun to canoodle with a local floosie! It explained the dishevelled blonde woman, who'd almost hit Ellen's hire car and swerved into the avenue of jacaranda trees just now. Ellen blushed deeply. Addan had been entertaining a woman—in *her* bedroom!

'Rats deserve drowning,' she muttered indignantly and glared at the blissfully oblivious man, cluttering up the huge antique bed, complicating her arrival. 'Rogue males like you I could do without!' she grumbled under her breath. 'Oh, drat you, Addan!'

A nasty surprise like this was too much after all the

7

hell she'd gone through after Bruno's death. Being widowed had been bad enough; the years before had been pretty strained, too. That was why she'd come for the first time to the island of Madeira. This house — once Bruno's, now hers — was supposed to be a refuge from all her troubles. Instead, one of the main causes of all her worries had turned up to make waves.

Her soft blue eyes lingered on the annoyingly perfect physique sprawled in possession of the bed, and her arm lowered. Addan was dangerously attractive. Even she, hating him as she did, wasn't immune to the incredible magnetism that had — according to Bruno — laid out women all over the world, horizontal and willing. Oh, yes. She knew all about Addan. Bruno had talked about his brother's legendary lust non-stop. The women, the callous two-timing, his pathological lies. . .

A capricious fate had built him like every girl's dream, and today it had decorously draped him in strategically placed emerald linen sheets as if he were posing for a *Playgirl* centrefold. Impossibly narrow hips and waist fanned out in a broadly muscled triangle to a pair of classically broad shoulders that would have made any female heart accelerate.

In the light shafting through the shutters, droplets of sweat gleamed in the dip of his back. The firm, satiny body tensed imperceptibly in some erotic sleeping paradise, and the sheet exposed a little more of his tight rear than was decent. She noticed — before tearing her eyes away — that he was dark honey-gold. *All over!*

A slight quiver disturbed her equilibrium at the thought of Addan sunning himself nude in her garden. Although she'd never set foot in the eighteenth-century mansion until ten minutes ago, what she'd seen had been breathtakingly beautiful and she'd fallen in love with it, running eagerly upstairs to freshen up and explore. Only to discover the shockingly naked Addan.

'Everywhere I go,' she whispered, 'you spoil my life.' On this magical garden island, in such an idyllic setting, she'd believed she could recover her shattered nerves at last—but not, she thought in despair, with Addan around, treating it like his personal naturist reserve!

'Well, Goldilocks,' she said decisively, determined to get rid of him fast. 'Time to wake up!'

But before she could pour the water one of his big, relaxed hands suddenly attached itself to her wrist, halting her arm in mid-air. A baleful black eye glowered at her as his sleep-tousled head lifted and the heavy eyebrows shot upwards in surprised recognition.

'Good lord! It's Mummy Bear!' His grip increased and his eyes glittered. 'You pour that at your peril,' he said in a deceptively soft warning, collecting his wits with barely a pause. 'And incidentally, if I'm anyone, I'm a wolf.' He gave a grin that proved it. 'And I like my fur dry in bed.'

Her heart began to thud hard but she stood her ground. Life had taught her self-protection, if nothing else. 'Oh, dear! Not Goldilocks?' she enquired drily.

'Not when I last looked,' mocked her brother-in-law, releasing her and pointedly adjusting the sheet around his pelvic bones.

She coloured up at the blatant sexual innuendo, her pulses picking up the rhythm of her heart—as they always did when Addan was around. There was something about him that always stepped up her awareness and made her adrenalin run. Because, of course, she knew that with him she needed to keep on her toes if she wasn't to be coaxed into sin.

'Wolf or not, you're still sleeping in *my* bed,' she complained, nonchalantly pouring herself a glass of water as if that had been her intention all along. Hiding her nerves, she took a sip, letting the ice-cold water lubricate her throat and moisten her dry lips.

Looking as cynical as ever, he drew himself up on one elbow. Ellen assumed a cool, distant expression and kept her gaze rigidly glued to his amused face. Addan might not care how much of his body he revealed, but she did!

'Your bed, eh?' he drawled. 'I think not. One of my

ancestors purchased this bed from a French sea captain in 1789. As far as I'm aware, this is the *master* bedroom. For the men of the house.'

She bristled. Trust Addan to take any opportunity to underline the difference between his aristocratic background and her council-house beginnings! 'Master bedroom? Isn't that a teensy bit old-fashioned?' she murmured.

'Not when I'm in it,' he said sardonically. 'Now unless you're planning on being mistress to my master I suggest you stake your claim on one of the minor beds in this house. Take your teddy and your baby-doll nightie and leave this one to me.'

'I will not. I own the house and everything in it,' she reminded him sweetly. 'And I want this bedroom.'

'Then. . .welcome,' he smiled, reaching down to lift the sheet invitingly.

'Without you in it!' she blazed suddenly. Drat him! she thought angrily, furious that he'd succeeded in riling her.

'Oh. You want me to get out?' A long, tanned and well-muscled leg shot out from under the covers and a bare foot touched down on the floor.

'No! Yes! Not now!' she snapped, appalled at the thought. 'I don't like seeing you dressed,' she went on icily, 'and the thought of you *undressed* turns my stomach. But when I go out in a moment I want you to get out of *my* bed. Then leave *my* house. And the island, for that matter,' she added as a grim afterthought. 'I doubt it's big enough for the two of us.'

'You always did have a singular lack of hospitality,' he said with a ghost of a smile. 'Funny how you get jumpy whenever I come near you.'

He spoke in the deep, intimate voice that always stole like a thief into her body. It was part of his 'adore me, I'm Addan' approach, she thought sourly, her heart hammering harder than ever.

'It's not funny at all,' she said calmly. 'There's a very

good reason. I'm extremely hospitable to guests who know how to behave——'

'Ahh,' he said with an innocence that was patently false. 'Got it! You want me to get drunk and throw someone in a swimming-pool and——'

Ellen gritted her teeth. 'Addan,' she said tightly, 'you walked in on a celebration that was getting out of hand through no fault of mine——'

'You let your friends treat you with such disrespect on your wedding-day?' he asked soberly.

She flushed. 'At least they didn't abuse my hospitality by. . .' She paused, wondering how to phrase it. Addan did it for her. He had fewer scruples.

'By trying to seduce you?' he suggested, his eyes dark and smouldering. 'You think that's why I'm here?'

'You tell me.'

Ellen faced him out, but felt a twinge of apprehension. He'd been trouble, even when fully dressed. Naked, in a bedroom, with a huge expanse of mattress waiting, he was quite unnervingly unpredictable. Guys like Addan should come with a health warning tattooed on their foreheads in ten-foot-high letters, she thought sourly. And took another sip of water to slake her dry throat.

There was a cynical expression on his face as he glanced from her moist lips to her blue eyes. 'All I did was kiss you,' he drawled. 'On that soft, lush mouth.' She tightened her soft, lush mouth into a grim line, and he smiled in an infuriatingly superior way. 'Kisses don't mean anything, do they? Not between relatives.'

'You did more than that! And in any case, it wasn't a relative kind of kiss,' she said, trying not to sound like an outraged virgin. 'And you know it. It was more a. . . coveting-your-brother's-wife kind of kiss.'

'I plead provocation, m'Lud,' he murmured.

'Me? Provocative?' she gasped, widening her eyes.

He shrugged his tan satin shoulders. Ellen found herself mesmerised by the extraordinary sensuality of his compelling eyes as they slowly studied her indignant face. 'Sure. You know how it's done. You've perfected it to a fine art. "How to challenge a jaded man and raise his blood-pressure",' he drawled. 'Look at you! Defiant, fiery, fearless, your face flushed, your skin glowing with anger, your body suffused with an energy I could touch — my sweet, sexy Ellen, you're provoking me even now.'

He licked his lips, reached for the glass and sipped speculatively, looking at her from under his brows. It was very erotic, and he probably knew it, she thought irritably.

'I'm not yours. I'm not sweet, I'm not sexy and you're talking nonsense!' she muttered huskily.

'You are the sexiest woman I've ever known,' he growled.

His eyes became serious and yearning, quite throwing her off balance. Literally; she rocked slightly on her feet and hastily said the first thing that came to mind.

'You're imag — imagin. . .' She stoped in dismay that she could stumble over such ordinary, casual words. Dismal failure!

'Very pretty,' he husked. 'Men can never resist vulnerable women.'

Ellen glowered, took a deep breath and started again, concentrating fiercely. 'I'm about as vulnerable,' she lied, 'as an armadillo ——'

'I think they have a soft spot under ——' he began helpfully.

'Oh! You know what I mean!' she snapped. 'It's no wonder I'm flushed! You annoy me so intensely that my blood's boiling!'

'Is that so?' he murmured in disbelief. 'Come on, Ellen, you were twisting men around your little finger at seventeen, when I first met you on that tea-boat in Amsterdam.'

'Met?' she queried indignantly. 'You burst into my cabin and ordered me to keep my grubby little paws off your brother! I'd hardly call that a meeting!'

'Explosive, wasn't it?' he mused. A slow crawling

flame crept over Ellen's cheeks. Explosive, she thought, her stomach churning. Nitro-glycerine just wasn't near it. 'You presented me with something of a problem,' Addan admitted softly. 'It was clear why he hadn't been able to resist you. I wasn't expecting anyone quite so. . .' his eyes plundered her body greedily '. . .gratuitously seductive.'

Her mouth fell open and she closed it again quickly, because his tongue had slid between his lips as if contemplating an opportunity. . . She tried frantically to concentrate on his latest insult. 'I was innocent of such things!' she protested. 'What did I know about seduction?'

'Quite a lot, from all accounts.'

She gave an impatient frown and wondered if Bruno had been boasting. It had been one of his failings. 'You read a lot more into an innocent woman's body-language than there actually was. Now if you don't mind I'm tired and——'

'That first kiss of ours,' he said quietly, 'almost rocked me off my feet. I wasn't mistaken about the powerful emotions behind it. It was something. . . special for you too, wasn't it?'

The warm Madeiran air seemed to thicken. Ellen felt the first surrendering of her body and took a steadying breath. But his low, butter-soft voice had all but collapsed her lungs.

'Yes,' she husked. 'It was.' She struggled to continue, to save her skin with a half-lie, half-truth. 'When you kissed me—your brother's girlfriend, for heaven's sake!—I began a loathing for you that has grown into an abiding hatred!'

'Hate? Don't you mean need? We can't forget the Seychelles the following year, can we?' he taunted, lifting a derisory eyebrow. 'Or perhaps it's usual in your set for a new bride to all but offer herself to another man on her wedding-day? Some quaint old custom maybe——'

Her eyes flashed with blue sparks. 'I did not offer myself!' she snapped. 'I'd only been married an hour!'

'Odd that you should go off for a swim, away from your new husband.'

Ellen tried not to remember, to blank out her mind. The ghastly celebration, with Bruno's lurching, drunken friends. . .'I was offshore and definitely off-limits,' she said stiffly. 'Just because I was swimming in a bikini didn't mean I was up for grabs by the likes of you!'

'No? The atmosphere was very conducive to sex. I remember a great deal of scurrying into palm groves while I was there,' he drawled.

She gazed at him helplessly. It had been the most unpleasant wedding she could ever have imagined. Oh, Bruno! she wailed inwardly. Why didn't you listen to me?

'I can't help that. Don't judge me by those people,' she said sharply.

'I'm afraid, Ellen,' he answered quietly, 'people *are* judged by the company they keep. The paparazzi called you. . .tacky, if I remember,' and he smiled icily when she winced. 'They pronounced your wedding an orgy. I wasn't too pleased to have my new sister-in-law making lurid headlines. It makes me wonder why you pretend to be bothered about a casual embrace. I would have thought a sophisticated woman like you would have taken that in her stride.'

Casual! she thought faintly. If that had been casual, what was he like when he was serious? His assault had been so complete that. . . She found her body weakening and steeled her senses.

'I did take it in my stride,' she replied coldly. 'I *strode* in the opposite direction as soon as I could escape your disgusting, groping hands.'

He smiled, apparently amused by her inaccurate description of his seamless, skilful move from antagonist to seducer. 'I'm impressed that you evidently managed to convince Bruno that our kiss was harmless,' he murmured. 'I thought he'd dump you after discovering us wrapped in passion against that palm tree.'

Her stomach somersaulted and she felt again the terrible sickness of that moment. 'I could have throttled you!' she grated hoarsely. 'Poor Bruno. . .' She said jerkily. 'What a vile revenge you took on us for disobeying you!'

'Didn't he doubt your devotion at all?' Addan growled, fixing her with a laser stare.

'Oh, you are evil!' she husked. 'Of course he did! You know how he felt about you! He lost all confidence in himself. He actually believed I was attracted to you! I wished you in hell on our wedding night!' she seethed, her blue eyes shot with angry lights. 'He was so upset. . .' Too late, she clapped a hand over her mouth at what she'd nearly said.

Addan's hands had curled into fists, his expanding chest warning her of his rising fury. 'God, is nothing sacred to you? Keep your bedroom secrets to yourself, you little tramp!' He snarled. 'I know I hurt him! You think I enjoyed that? But I'd have done anything to steer him clear of you and improve his life by getting rid of you; any way, any how! I wish I could have reached you too and made you suffer, but nothing much touches your emotions, does it, Ellen?'

She stared at him mutely. He didn't know. He had no idea of the depth of her trauma. But now, for the first time, he was revealing the depth of his hatred for her.

'So,' he growled, 'you can stride away again and leave me here. I'm going to put my head down for a few hours. I've flown six thousand miles without sleep ——'

'Why?' she asked warily.

With some difficulty, he reined in his anger and Ellen realised how much in control of himself he was. 'I can never sleep on planes.' A wry quirk lifted the sharply sculpted lips. 'Lack of a cuddly Mummy Bear to send me to dreamland, do you think?'

Her breath was drawn in to show her exasperation, but it only served to bring his predatory gaze to her clinging top as the magenta jersey expanded with her rising breasts. Ellen tried desperately to control her breathing in case he thought she was being provocative again.

'This is no dream, it's a nightmare! Now I know why they're called *Grimm's Fairy Tales*,' she said tartly, 'with the emphasis definitely on the grim!'

His mouth twitched a little more. 'Your wit's improved. So are your clothes. Quite a change from the widow's weeds you were wearing the last time we met, isn't it?' he marvelled, pretending mock-wonder at her tangerine button-through skirt stylishly open to the thighs and the tight scarlet leggings beneath.

'Colour therapy,' she snapped. Addan's brow crooked up curiously and she could have bitten her tongue out. 'To cheer up the Customs officers and divert their attention from my luggage,' she added with a knowing smile that suggested she'd smuggled in some illicit essentials.

To her relief, he bought her explanation — maybe because he thought she was a clothes-horse, and a shallow little airhead. Ellen knew that she'd have to stick with that ghastly bit of characterisation. At the moment, her emotions were fragile and vulnerable and Addan mustn't know that or he'd gladly do all he could to hurt her.

Indulging his salacious hunger thoroughly, he let his glance examine every inch of her brightly clothed body. 'Delightful. You're like an Amazonian parrot,' he mused. 'And how long your legs are! I never realised they went up that far.'

She tweaked her skirt so that it came to rest more demurely over her legs. The action helped to hold down her mounting agitation. 'You never really saw *me* at all,' she said with asperity.

'Didn't I?' he murmured, a sliver of contempt lacing his voice. 'I have twenty-twenty vision. I know what I saw: trouble for my brother. A flirty-eyed hippie in stylish rags ——'

'I was broke!' she protested. 'It's hard to get an apartment in Amsterdam. I couldn't get work ——'

'You didn't have to,' he said smoothly. 'Not with my naïve brother eager to be your meal-ticket.' He raised mocking eyes to heaven. 'And the fool thought he had to marry you!'

'You know he loved me!' she cried, finally goaded by his mockery. 'How *dare* you call him a fool? How can you talk about him like that now he's dead? If Bruno was unworldly, it was your fault for dominating him for most of his life!'

Addan stared, revealing his intense dislike in every line of his face. 'My brother was far too uncritical, Ellen. Even you must admit that. He made some disastrous friendships.' He let his gaze flick up and down her body again insolently. 'I should never have given him his head. The moment I did, a scheming little madam got her hands on him!'

Despite his even tone, his look would have curled steel. Ellen tried to calm her tattered nerves. 'You've said all this before, dozens of times,' she said as calmly as she could. 'You think I'm trash; I think you're a vicious and unprincipled bully. Let's leave it at that.'

Despite her spirited defence, she was already feeling the doubts and the guilt about Bruno's death flooding through her, weakening her ability to stand up to Addan's brutally insistent attacks on her character. They'd met four times: Amsterdam, her wedding, that time Bruno first was ill, and then his funeral. Each time, Addan's intense and deliberate projection of animal desire had unnerved her. And they'd quarrelled on each occasion, till she felt limp and raw.

'For a supposedly sweet, innocent widow, you seem singularly lacking in alarm at being alone in a bedroom with a naked man. Doesn't my lack of clothes bother you?' he asked with deceptive mildness.

She scowled, knowing she was damned if she said yes, damned if she said no. 'It's the principle of having my personal privacy violated that I object to,' she said, stiffly pompous. 'It's overriding anything else I might have felt. You can't just barge into this house when you please! It's mine and you're not welcome. Get dressed and go!'

Addan smoothed back his glossy hair, taming the wayward, sexy black curls with impatient sweeps of his hands. Even without the aid of expensively tailored suits, she thought resentfully, he still looked like an autocratic steel baron who snacked on defenceless women with his oysters and champagne.

'What exactly are you doing in Madeira?' he rapped suddenly.

Running! she almost blurted out. Escaping from the past. 'It seemed a nice place to come,' she answered vaguely, tightening up her shaky defences. Lack of concentration could be fatal when Addan was around, she thought gloomily. 'Bruno's house had been left to me; I thought I'd make use of it for a little holiday.' Did that sound simpering enough? she wondered.

His glance darted quickly around the room as if he expected to see things missing. Ellen resentfully followed his gaze to the dusty Flemish paintings and the Madeiran landscapes of dramatic ravines and cascading waterfalls but her interest in the French-furnished bedroom was secondary to her anxiety.

Her stomach swooped. Maybe Addan had an inkling of Bruno's financial disaster and that was why he'd come. She dreaded him ever finding out! He'd tear her apart with his bare hands and then sell the pieces for dog food.

'Been here before?' he asked warily, still continuing his mental inventory.

'Never. You know how it is, with Longchamps and Monte Carlo and the Paris collections,' she said sarcastically, wondering what he'd do if he ever heard the truth.

'Oh, God!' he sighed, raising his eyes to the ceiling.

'And if you're worried about what's missing, I've just this minute arrived.' She felt deeply offended by his suspicious attitude. 'I haven't had time to check over the family silver, let alone crate it up and sell it,' she scathed, as if the idea was ridiculous. That should put him off the scent!

The imperious gaze slowly swept up her body in a fluttering of heavy black lashes. 'How very fortunate for you,' he said, with soft menace.

The threat hung in the air between them. To avoid being scalded alive by his vicious eyes, she fiddled with the cluster of pearls which dangled from her ears and struggled for calm.

His vengeance was legendary. She'd heard the fear in Bruno's voice when he'd begged her not to let Addan know that half the Torre fortune had been lost. Under that smooth, civilised exterior Addan affected lay a wild flame of temper and the determination of an ox. She thought of the way he'd single-mindedly chased her and Bruno all over Europe, trying to prevent their marriage: how he'd bribed and lied and cheated in the attempt to reach them in time.

And she thought of the revenge he'd taken, the carefully calculated embrace that had shattered Bruno's manhood. Addan was quite ruthless. She shivered, and turned it into a casual brushing of her scarlet knee, as if there were a fleck of cotton there. Her instincts told her to take a step back, out of the range of the bed and Addan's powerful arms, but she knew that attack was her only defence if she was to maintain some dignity.

'Maybe *you're* here to run off with a few mementoes,' she suggested in a brittle voice.

'If I'd wanted to empty this house of all the possessions my family has collected over the last few centuries,' he said tightly, 'I'd have driven up in an articulated lorry and removed the lot. I don't do anything by halves.'

No, she thought shakily. She'd noticed. Forcing a pleasant smile to her face, she said sweetly; 'Perhaps you'd explain why you *are* here.'

'I like to travel.'

'Ever thought of outer space?' she asked irritably, and regretted blurting out such a catty, unworthy remark, with all her heart.

He flinched and anger glittered in his dark eyes. 'Oh, yes,' he said coldly. 'Often. I dream of a rocket carrying you at the speed of light towards a Black Hole.'

Annoyed with herself for losing composure, Ellen turned her back on him and stalked over the heavy-weight dust sheet to open the shutters, wishing her skirt wouldn't dance quite so pertly behind her.

'Bruno would be upset to know we were quarrelling like this,' she said huskily, struggling with the iron latch.

'Bruno's dead.'

She winced at the unemotional tone. 'His memory isn't,' she said, an infinite sadness making her words sound harsh.

'I bet. You spent four years of your life with him clinging to your brief little skirts.'

'Addan!' she gasped, her hand falling limply from the latch.

'It's true, isn't it?' he muttered. 'I suppose the last year has been quite a release for you. You've been fancy-free, able to do whatever you like.' He paused as if awaiting some response from her. She remained silent, thinking of the awesome burden of responsibilities that had been heaped on her shoulders, and he continued. 'My memory of Bruno goes back a longer way than yours.'

She jerked her head around to look at him, alerted by the depth of emotion in his voice. And wished she hadn't. There was a blistering hostility in his eyes that would have sliced her in two if it were physically possible.

'I know how intense his relationship was with you,' she said in a low tone.

'You two should never have got together,' he growled.

Ellen struggled with the part of her that agreed. 'Spilt

milk,' she said sadly. 'It's done. Over. Oh, Addan, why do we always fight over him?' she sighed.

'Is that what you think this is?' he asked slowly.

'Of course, what else?' she asked in surprise. 'Look, Addan, we both loved him—but in totally different ways——'

'You for his money, I because we were of the same flesh and blood.'

Ellen looked at him helplessly. 'There you go again!' she said unhappily. 'No wonder you bring out the worst in me! I feel like an Aunt Sally in a fairground when you're around, constantly dodging everything you throw at me! I'm not sharp-tongued with anyone else!'

'That's because no one else sees through your bright chatter to the selfish creature beneath,' he said callously. 'I was the only one who fought your marriage— and you weren't used to being thwarted, were you? Your coaxing little ways hide quite a street-wise, devious determination. Despite your apparently bubbling scattiness, I've seen that vivacious face of yours turn in microseconds to a steely determination.'

She sighed, wearying of the eternal battle. 'I can be strong when necessary,' she agreed huskily. 'Like when I think there's a serious injustice. I wish I knew why you took an instant dislike to me.'

'Because my seventeen-year-old brother said he was going to marry a penniless girl,' he said quietly.

'Didn't his feelings come into it?' she cried. 'You forced us to go on the run. And wasn't it a bit strong, persuading the Turkish police to help you by accusing Bruno of stealing from you?'

His eyes looked lethal. 'I'll use any means, any means at all, to get what I want,' he said softly.

'Then you're a danger to society,' she snapped. Anger thinned her mouth and she turned to open the window, taking in deep breaths of fresh air. Dangerous? Addan was like the serpent in the Garden of Eden. And she and Bruno had been condemned to roam a spiritual wilderness.

Her hands gripped the mahogany windowsill. Glorious spring sunshine warmed her tense, pale face and she lifted it to the healing warmth, trying to get a hold on herself.

Outside was a paradise. Feeling depressed that it was being ruined, she looked down on the veranda roof swamped by rampant scarlet bougainvillaea and to the subtropical garden beyond, its lawns decorated by imposing palms and stands of ancient dragon trees. Two doves fluttered on to a branch of a mimosa tree, bright with yellow blossom. They began to coo prettily to one another. Wistfully, Ellen watched them pursue their courtship in the boughs of a cherry orchard.

Her spirits lifted a little. Across the valley, vineyards patterned the lower terraces of the steep hills which were backed by a wall of snow-capped mountains. Yes. She'd been right to come, she decided. Now she must get rid of the Satan who'd invaded this earthly Eden.

'Addan,' she said huskily, feeling soothed by the tranquil scene and able to face him boldly again, 'there's too much hostility between us to share this house — or even Madeira itself. To be honest, I doubt either of us would be happy even in the same half of the globe. You have the whole of Brazil to strut around in —'

'Sure I have. But this is my home,' he said softly.

'Your home?' she stiffened. There was a suitcase near her feet. Her voice hardened in desperation. 'Keep off my territory!' she warned shakily.

He frowned. 'Your territory!' he scathed. 'You don't deserve to own the Quinta! What the hell do you know, or care, about its history? Have you any sense of heritage? God, I dread to think of the changes you'll make! Jacuzzis, I suppose,' he said scornfully. 'Modern plastic baths in avocado-green, fancy kitchen units —'

'Wrong again! I know the history of this house — and the island,' she replied with a quiet passion. 'Bruno made me promise. . .' Her teeth dug into her lower lip.

She'd almost given herself away. 'He wanted me to come here,' she said with more caution. Addan's technique of getting people mad and thus hearing the truth was infuriating! 'And you have completely misjudged my character. You know nothing of me or my life with Bruno ——'

'Unfortunately I do,' he frowned. 'Extravagant champagne parties, the boring, glittering social circuit. . . It's always the same — you as much as admitted it yourself. Gstaad for skiing, New York to shop, Cannes for the film festival, Wimbledon, Ascot. A shallow, empty life for a shallow, empty woman,' he said, his scathing tongue lashing cruelly.

Ellen checked her denial, feeling tears of self-pity welling up. It would break her heart to talk about what had really happened: the whole ghastly story. She was so much on edge, so near to breaking-point that she couldn't speak about the awful time she'd had, or the catastrophic past year since Bruno had died. Addan would probably be glad to hear she was at a low ebb — and he'd never believe her, anyway. Besides, the last thing she wanted to do in front of Addan was to cry.

'Whatever your opinion of me,' she said quietly, 'you have to accept the situation. I own the Quinta das Magnolias. You have no right to use this house as a pit-stop.' Thinking of what he'd been doing, within hours of landing, she was unable to stop her voice shaking with distress and anger. 'Or as a temporary whore-house!' she said in trembling outrage over her shoulder. 'How *dare* you?'

'*Deus*! You offend my honour ——!'

'Honour? What honour?' she retorted sharply. 'No man who tries to seduce his sister-in-law could ——'

'That's enough!' he roared, making her cringe.

She saw he was about to scramble out of bed and spun hastily on her heel to gaze in wide-eyed alarm out of the window, seeing nothing. His bare feet crossed the room in a couple of strides. He stopped inches from her and she could feel the heat of his body radiating out as if an electric current had been passed over her skin, lifting all her nerve-endings and making her agitation worse. Oh, God! she thought, pressing herself to the window in panic. He was mother-naked!

# CHAPTER TWO

ELLEN'S entire body trembled with tension. 'Move away!' she demanded sharply. 'Have you no shame?'

'Absolutely none,' he gritted. 'We have that much in common, don't we?'

'We have *nothing* in common!'

Ellen itched to slap him — but she dared not turn around. He knew that, keeping her a virtual prisoner at the window while she pretended to be unaffected by the electrifyingly virile man standing an inch or so away from her straining body.

She noticed that the doves had flown. Instead, an eagle soared on thermals above the valley, quartering the verdant terraces for its prey. Her sympathies were with the unsuspecting rabbits.

Hold on, she told herself. Don't crack. He'd be thrilled.

'There are two things we have in common. Bruno for one,' he said softly in her ear.

His hands came to rest on the window-ledge on either side of her, the muscles in his bare arms flexed as if tensed for action. Gulping, her body throbbing alarmingly, she tore her eyes from the strong sinews and gazed blindly ahead.

'We don't even belong to the same human race,' she said wildly.

'You vicious little bitch!' he growled. 'You're as ruthless as I am. That's the other thing we share. Unwavering determination. We both know what we want and how to get it, no matter what the cost. The only difference is that I have a code of honour and you don't. It's precious to me,' he seethed, his hot breath rasping her cheek. 'Don't malign my honour, or I promise you, Ellen, I'll squeeze you till the pips squeak

and engage in a battle of wills with you that'll make the
Greek wars look like a vicarage bunfight!'

Menace chilled the blood in her veins till it seemed to
run at half its usual speed. In a gesture of defiance, she
tossed back the heavy chestnut fall of hair that had
swung forwards over her face.

'Intimidation doesn't work on me,' she lied coldly,
propping up her trembling legs by forcing them hard
against the wall. 'My father was a bouncer in a nightclub
and I know all the tricks you men use. And I've been
around, too. I'm not impressed.'

'You should be,' he growled. 'I don't make idle
threats. Most people realise that and run like hell. But
then, you have little sense in that pretty little head,' he
said patronisingly. 'Even Bruno admitted you were
something of a marshmallow-brain and as arrogant and
thick-skinned as an armadillo!'

'My, the insults are flying thick and fast,' she murmured, trying not to let him provoke her. He was lying
about Bruno, she thought scornfully, though it was just
as well he didn't knew how thin-skinned she was. At
this very moment her legs were wobbling as if she'd
been on a frightening fairground ride. 'But if I am as
tough as old boots, then doesn't it occur to you that
perhaps you've met your match at last?'

'Not at all,' he said silkily. 'I very much doubt that
anyone is more arrogant or thick-skinned than I.'

'Then I'd better put my demand plainly so it gets
through your thick skin. I want you to go,' she
repeated, her mouth grim. '*Now.*'

'Persistent woman! I'm staying. I came here for a
little peace,' he drawled infuriatingly.

Peace! Oh, she'd longed for that, for longer than she
cared to remember. Her intention had been to camp
out in Bruno's old family home — no matter what its
condition — since 'it was the only refuge she had. She
certainly didn't want any more business hassles,
emotional scenes or reminders of the past.

Ellen bit her lip. For the last couple of months, she'd

been unconsciously winding down. It was unfortunate that she'd begun to release some of her tight control, anticipating a life of peaceful solitude on the beautiful island. Alone, in the privacy of the Quinta, she had meant to let go at last and have a good howl. That was now impossible, she thought in despair. Now she had to strap on her armour again and do battle. To hell with his peace! she thought resentfully. What about hers?

'I have no intention of giving any favours to the man who tried to ruin his own brother's happiness,' she said through her teeth. Why did he always interfere? Her hands formed into fists, the long nails digging painfully into her palms.

'If you're preparing to launch that slender fist in the direction of my jaw, forget it,' he said laconically. 'I'd resist, and we'd end up in an undignified struggle on the floor and then——'

'Hit you? Oh, no! That would mean *touching* you!' Ellen shuddered, appalled at the thought of contact with that warm, flawless skin, of being wrapped in those powerful, naked limbs. Her nerves were screaming. She ached from standing so rigidly, her whole body ready to burst with a barely leashed anger. 'Haven't you understood yet? You're utterly repellent to me! For God's sake, go!' she cried hoarsely over her shoulder.

There was a tense silence. Ellen's heart sank. She'd attacked his male vanity, the very thing he held most precious. All his life he'd been proud. Everyone had admired him, fearing but idolising the devastatingly handsome, tough heir to the Torre wealth. Quiet, reticent Bruno had been virtually ignored. Addan had risen like scum to the top, and expected worship as his due.

The hairs on the back of her neck lifted with his sharp, quick breathing and she realised he was controlling his temper with enormous difficulty. She could sense his rage, visualise the hard contours of his golden chest rising and falling, the ruthless, determined mouth thinning to a stubborn line. Her body tightened till every inch of it hurt with the strain. He'd make her regret her words, she thought in panic. Starting now.

'So you really hate me that much,' he said softly. A finger touched the side of her neck and she flinched away from it with a shuddering gasp of fear. Definitely fear, she told herself in faint alarm. 'I always wondered what your exact feelings were,' murmured Addan, almost unnervingly controlled.

'I thought I'd made that plain.'

'Not really. Sometimes I thought that you harboured an unholy passion for me.' He paused and she could feel him breathing. In. Out. In. Out. She found herself holding her breast, to assuage the tight ache there. 'But that's silly, isn't it?' he drawled.

'Yes,' she said, her mouth strangely dry.

His breath exhaled, riffling her hair, and she wanted to scream. He knew just how to intimidate people, she thought bitterly. He'd have made a champion bouncer! Something of Ellen's indomitable spirit returned. She'd outface this autocratic Madeiran somehow. Her body relaxed a little ——

And leapt into a thousand pieces again as his hand rested lightly on her back. She could feel the strength in that hand, the controlled pressure, the unusually large area it was able to span. Her breath was steaming up the window so that she couldn't see out, but she still stared blindly ahead, wishing her ribcage wouldn't heave so obviously.

'You know,' he said in a low, conversational tone that was terrifyingly sinister, 'if I were a really vindictive man, I could push you through this pane of glass.'

Ellen's whole body stilled as if it had been frozen. Could he smell the fear that came from her? Sweat prickled her palms and she wiped them on her hips. A longer, deeper exhalation behind her made it clear that he'd seen, noted and was pleased at her apprehension.

'A little drastic,' she said breathily. 'I'm not worth the effort of clearing up the mess, surely?'

He chuckled and removed his hand. 'Tough little cookie, aren't you?' he said with grudging admiration. 'And since you are, and nothing much bothers you, then you can at least let me sleep for an hour or two. I'm dog-tired. Virtually sleep-walking.'

'Then I *was* right about the blonde who came hurtling out of here when I turned up!' she exclaimed, instantly annoyed, her face pink at the thought of him in bed with the woman, embracing her. . .

'Ellen, you were not!' he snapped, evidently touchy about the subject. 'You didn't see Maria, understand?'

'I did!' she countered grimly, still hypnotised by the image of Addan's strong mouth skimming over the blonde's shoulders. . .

Roughly, he turned her around. Her gaze flicked briefly downwards in horror and he seemed amused by her patent relief that his lean hips were decently draped in the green sheet. But he wasn't diverted for long, and increased his grip on her, drawing her attention back to his glowing, coal-black eyes.

'You will *never* tell anyone that she was here while I was here, in this bedroom,' he muttered.

Her eyes searched his, puzzled. What did he care about a woman's reputation? Then she realised that he didn't. He cared for his own. 'Oh, Addan!' she cried, aghast. 'Do you mean she's married?'

'Very,' he growled. Her eyes widened in distress. 'Don't pretend to be shocked,' he said impatiently. 'I know the bed-hopping set you ran with, remember?' She shrugged him off crossly, her eyes temporarily mesmerised by the great spread of his chest and its triangle of curling black hairs. Too close, her pulses were saying. They were too close. 'Now be a good girl and swear you'll keep your mouth shut,' he insisted.

Ellen snapped her mind back. 'Oh, don't worry,' she retorted in contempt. 'Your promiscuity is your problem, not mine. I have no intention of destroying some unfortunate man's faith in his adulterous wife.'

Addan grunted and his hands ran down her arms

lightly, making her insides buck. 'You think she's your sister under the skin?' he frowned. 'That you share something in common with each other?'

'What do you mean?' she asked, bewildered.

He gave her a mocking smile and sauntered back to the high antique bed, propping pillows against the elaborately carved walnut headboard and lounging against them like a Roman god, his hair intensely black and the deep South American tan quite stunning against the beautiful linen.

'Interesting that you automatically assume that she's an opportunist, hunting wealthy men for what she can get,' he mused. 'Now why? Because that's what you do and you assume all women behave like that?'

'I didn't — !'

'You damn well did!' he interrupted. 'Forget any comparison. She doesn't have your chillingly calculating mind.'

'I'm not — !' she began indignantly.

'She's in love with me,' he interrupted again, with astonishing frankness. 'Has been for years. So leave her alone.'

Ellen's breath caught in her throat and she clutched at the heavy brocade drapes with trembling fingers. For some reason, that information had taken her unawares, making her pulses race as if she'd been in a marathon.

'I see. . .' Her mind whirled. It sounded like a long-standing affair. Addan in love! Was this why he was so bitter, and sought solace in women-by-numbers? 'You — you've been in love with a married woman for years?'

A faint smile touched his white lips. 'I suppose I have,' he said quietly.

'Oh, how sad!' she said with genuine sorrow. 'What are you going to do?' For several seconds, he locked eyes with her, as if making up his mind. 'Addan,' she said unhappily, 'leave her! There'll be another woman —'

'No,' he said with finality. His haunted, bleak face

tugged at her heart and her eyes grew soft with tender
compassion. There was an answering despair in the
melting darkness of his glowing eyes that made her
clasp her hands to prevent her from extending them to
him in comfort.

'There will,' she said shakily. 'Another woman will
come along——'

'Like a number ninety-eight bus? Love doesn't work
like that, Ellen, not for me. You, skimming along the
surface of life like a pond-skater, wouldn't ever begin
to understand. I'm a one-woman man,' he said with
chilling finality. 'I've given all my heart, all my soul.
There's nothing left to give anyone else. I don't take
second-best.'

'Does this mean you're going to fight for her?' she
asked miserably, wondering why she felt as if he'd
emptied the life from her body with his revelation.

To her astonishment, he gave a cynical smile. 'I mean
to have whatever I can,' he said softly. 'Anything I can
get.'

'Sex,' she said unhappily, her emotions churning.

'Why not?' he husked. 'I'm devoured by an insatiable
lust, Ellen. Women like you don't know what it's like to
have an obsession, to feel passions so fierce that they
threaten all reason.'

'Oh, Addan!' she whispered, her heart touched by
his plight. 'You're strong-minded—don't let it take
over your life! Think of this woman's husband——'

'What? Oh. . .' He gave a mirthless laugh. 'Don't
worry, Ellen. I don't break up marriages,' he said flatly.

'You had a good go at mine!' she blurted out
accusingly.

His dark, steady gaze seemed to melt into her like a
knife through butter. 'That was different,' he growled.
'You and Bruno were unsuited to one another. I wanted
to save you both from heartache——'

'Oh, how very kind!' she cried, furious that she'd
wasted her compassion on him. He was a manipula-
tor—and had probably been angling for her sympathy

for some ulterior motive. 'How dare you play God?
Why don't you just admit that you couldn't bear Bruno
to make choices of his own without you? That you
hated the idea of a woman showing no interest in you at
all —— '

'I wouldn't say *that* was true,' he drawled.

She trembled visibly, impaled by his serious black
eyes, resenting the fact that he'd kissed her. And
furious that she'd never been able to forget the terrible,
carnal sensations of lust and hunger he'd briefly aroused
in her. She'd been faced with passions that she didn't
want to own.

Especially that time in the Seychelles. She'd swum
far out to get away from the scenes on the beach that
had made her want to cry. Addan had appeared beside
her in the warm, enveloping water, wrapping his limbs
around her and driving his mouth into hers so brutally,
so hungrily that she'd been taken unawares. And for a
brief moment, desperately needing comfort, she had
responded and he'd refused to listen to her pleas after
that, but had laid siege to her body with a ruthless
determination that made her forget everything.

'You self-opinionated devil! I told you, I hate you!'
she whispered with heartfelt fervour, desperate to shut
away the memory forever.

'Is that so?' He smiled faintly, his eyes never leaving
hers for an instant. Unwillingly, she absorbed into her
pores the power he was projecting, a compelling, silent
call that she heard in the core of her body, the depths of
her bemused brain. Heard it; felt helplessly driven to
obey it. 'Come here, Ellen,' he said in a husky murmur.

She swayed forwards but desperately pulled herself
back, her feet rooted to the floor. Men had tried to
seduce her dozens of times. None had ever got as close
as Addan. Her eyes closed in humiliation that he could
still arouse the wanton, primitive part of her she
preferred to keep buried. Then her eyes snapped wide
open again.

He'd had a reason to seduce her then. He probably

had a reason to try now. Male hunger. Or pride that his record of success had been broken by her refusal to contemplate leaping into bed with him. A woman unconquered. And he could do this, even while loving someone else!

'One of these days,' she said bitterly, 'I'm going to recommend you for open-heart surgery.'

'There's nothing wrong with my heart.'

'Yes, there is,' she said locking her gaze with his in bold defiance. 'It's absent. You need one put in!'

He laughed unexpectedly, and she felt her whole body weaken because it was the first time she'd ever seen his face look so warm and appealing. No wonder women admired him, she thought in confusion. He must be quite devastating when he chose to exert his easy charm. She thought of the eagle and hardened her heart. Far too many people lately had made her their victim.

'What a challenge you are to the male ego! And quite extraordinarily beautiful,' he said softly, his eyes making liquid out of her bones. 'Like a flamboyant butterfly in those eye-catching clothes. Sparkling, daring, undaunted. You'd dazzle any man with your vibrance. I don't blame you for using your beauty to advance yourself.' For the second time, he lifted a corner of the sheet invitingly, exposing a length of muscular gold thigh. 'Come here,' he husked. 'Let me show you what being rich is really like.'

His soft, honeyed voice could have stolen her senses if she didn't know what a rat he was. 'I don't barter my body for money,' she said, her voice strangely husky.

'Bank account full, is it? Then what will you barter your body for?' he murmured.

'Love,' answered Ellen proudly, sadness in her expression that Bruno had never taken what she had willingly offered. Her body, her love.

Addan gave a derisory laugh. 'Are you winding me up?' he asked. 'Listen, sweetheart, if you thought to disarm me with your cloying sentimentality, you can think again. Besides, love is the one price I would never pay for you.'

'I'd never ask you to,' she countered grimly.

'What a pity. It looks as though I'll have to snuggle down without the company of Mummy Bear.'

'Wasn't that a grim fairy tale?' she muttered.

He gave a wintry smile. 'I'd forgotten. My childhood was shorter than most. Twelve-year-old heads of multi-national organisations get balance sheets, not fairy-stories at bedtime.'

'If you're trying to make me feel sorry for you——' she said irritably, feeling an unwelcome twinge of just that.

'Not at all. I think you should remember that I was thrown into the real world to sink or swim with the sharks at an age when childen are worrying about maths tests and getting into the soccer team.' His eyes gleamed. 'My sexual awakening came early too.'

'Well, I think you should put it to sleep,' she muttered.

'I intend to. Sleep is about all that's left at this moment, isn't it?'

He slid down in the big French bed and his long black lashes descended to lie on his broad cheekbones. Ellen frowned, quite disconcerted, wondering what to do. But his words had reminded her of the reason he was so arrogant and why he had a tendency to do whatever he pleased with no regard for others.

His parents had died in a hit-and-run accident on a remote Brazilian road. She'd heard all about that, from Bruno; how Addan had struggled to assert himself over the powerful company directors and then to take the reins of the Torre businesses; how he'd single-mindedly abandoned childhood pleasures to stamp his mark on everyone. Bruno included.

She studied the strong-boned faced thoughtfully. Addan had been old before his time and yet too young to realise that love should be behind all discipline. Poor Bruno—ruled with a rod of inflexible iron! No wonder he'd become insecure and timid. She sighed. Addan was — what? — twenty-nine? His habit of bullying people into submission was probably ingrained.

But she loathed him believing that he'd twisted *her* around his little finger. 'I'll bring a teddy to your cell in Funchal,' she told him drily. 'If I can't find a friendly woodcutter who chops the heads off stray wolves, I'm going to get the police.' She strode determinedly to the door.

'Unwise,' came Addan's voice. Its menacing drawl stopped her in her tracks.

'Because?' she enquired haughtily.

'There would be a scandal.'

Her eyes widened. 'Why?'

'Family unity is important here. I won't have the local people here thinking that members of my family are at war with one another.'

'Oh, don't be ridiculous ——' she began, half turning.

'My family is above reproach!' he roared, making her jump and eye him warily. 'They are united in public, no matter what. That, Ellen, is why I was so furious when I heard about your adventures, when they were plastered across the society pages in the national Press. You brought the respected name of Torre into disrepute and that was unforgiveable!'

'It wasn't my ——'

'Eject me by force,' he snarled, 'before I'm ready to go, and I'll contact every damn paparazzo in the business!'

'You'll *what*?' she gasped, whirling fully around in a blur of orange and scarlet.

He smiled unpleasantly. 'Your name is already mud. I can do nothing about that. But involve me personally in your eventful life and I will take action. The widow of the tragically young, jet-setting Bruno Machico de Torre is still hot news,' he said tightly, unleashing all his malevolent spite on her. 'You make a good centre-fold. Reporters and photographers will descend in their hordes.'

She blanched at the thought of a Press invasion. The glare of publicity would be unbearable — and what if the Press found out what she'd been doing. . .? Worse, supposing Addan got to hear of it? She gritted her teeth. He had her beaten. For now.

'Bastard is too good a word for you,' she muttered fervently. 'I do wish my vocabulary were wider.'

'Surely you picked up a few choice expressions while mingling with the foul-mouthed Euroset?' he murmured insolently.

Tiredness washed over her limbs. She wanted to collapse into a hot bath and stay there till morning. 'Leave it, Addan!' Her hand pushed back the heavy drop of hair in a distracted gesture. 'Don't you think we hurled enough abuse at each other over Bruno's grave?' she asked, white-lipped.

Addan's jaw tightened, but the eyes that looked at her seemed deep and haunted. 'I was justified,' he said quietly. 'You drove him to his death.'

'Oh, no,' she moaned.

The taunt pierced her body like a twisting knife. And with the anguish came a shame that stained her face a slow crimson as she tried desperately to forget the awful scene at the funeral. It was a year ago. Past history. And she'd been distraught, worn to the bone from nursing Bruno twenty-four hours a day.

'Oh, yes,' he growled. 'It's not surprising that I exploded with anger then. I was incensed with your selfish behaviour, forcing him to take you to parties when he was so ill!' His voice rose. 'You're lucky I didn't push you in the grave and bury you with him!'

'Addan! *Please*!' she wailed, her eyes filling with tears.

'I'll never forgive you for accelerating his death!' he seethed. 'I have a depth of passion for people I love that you couldn't even begin to appreciate. What was your excuse for screaming at me like a fishwife?'

Total despair. Terrible regrets.

Ellen swayed with the lacerating pain tearing at her

body. He'd pushed her too far once again and she had to get out of the room. He'd given her a means to do so. 'I won't discuss it,' she whispered harshly. 'All right. Sleep — if your conscience allows. You've got an hour. No more.'

He glowered, but to her relief his smudge-dark lids closed. 'That'll do. I recover quickly. It's the secret of my success.'

She hoped her filthy look would penetrate his thick skin and poison him like a curare-tipped dart, but, ignorant of it, he merely turned over, presenting the great panorama of his smooth back to her. It seemed rigid, as if he was waiting for her to go.

'I'll be downstairs,' she croaked.

Her legs wobbled when she moved but she couldn't get out fast enough. Shutting the ornately carved bedroom door firmly behind her, she slumped wearily against it, incapable of taking another step. Gone was her intention to lie down and relax. She remained helplessly on the darkened landing, emotionally spent, restless and disorientated.

'Oh, hell!' she groaned. How would she hold herself together for an hour? Addan's presence made any relaxing impossible.

That bath would have been soothing, but she certainly wasn't taking any clothes off when he was around. He'd never acknowledged any reason to control his sexual impulses. All women were potential conquests to him, a challenge to his masculinity.

She didn't want to think of her own near-surrender; it had been too humiliating. But, as if to torment her, the images kept coming. . .

She: seventeen, nervous of meeting Bruno's fabled brother for the first time, reeling in shock at Addan's revelation that Bruno was very wealthy. Then defying the ultimatum Addan had given her to leave Bruno alone or regret it for ever more.

As she had, and always would.

He: filling the untidy cabin with his searing scorn and

an unsettling virility, his coaxing voice becoming silkier and softer with every second, his eyes mesmeric, sensual. Till the atmosphere had become unbreathable, her body hot and prickling with bewildering sensations.

Ellen shuddered. She remembered as if it were yesterday that moment when he'd broken the unbearable spell and caught her to him like a rag doll, kissing her with a fierce, desperate passion that had torn all seven veils from her sleeping sexuality and almost made her respond with equal abandon. Innocent, untutored, she'd been stunned by Addan's devastating knowledge of the art of seduction as he'd masterfully caressed her body. But something had saved her. Just in time, she'd realised what Addan was doing — and why.

Shaking uncontrollably even now, Ellen stumbled forwards to grip the dusty newel post at the top of the stairs. And with a desperate effort she tried to fight down the wilful resurgence of her wayward sexual needs. Dizziness swept over her, but it wasn't like the vertigo she usually felt when faced with heights. It was a spinning in her head, brought on by humiliating memories of her shameful physical vulnerability to Addan.

Oh, his passion had been real enough — the lust of a man who thought women were created purely for pleasure. He'd been utterly confident in his own mind that she'd opt for him instead of the reserved seventeen-year-old Bruno. A man instead of a boy.

Her breath shuddered at the anguish she'd felt after she'd raged like a banshee at the surprised Addan. That anger had been directed at herself. God forgive her, she knew that in her heart of hearts she'd betrayed Bruno because she'd desired his brother — however briefly — and her feelings for Bruno had been tarnished forever.

How *could* she? Even to compare the two men. . . Her eyes glittered coldly. Addan had set out to seduce his brother's girl — no matter what she'd looked like — to prove to Bruno that she didn't love him at all. That was evil — and what was more he'd repeated the trick every time he could get near her.

She felt nauseous, but forced herself to go downstairs, away from the man she despised. 'Oh, God!' she whispered, sitting down hard on the bottom step. Bruno had idolised her. Supposing she'd surrendered to her instincts, and let Addan make love to her? Bruno would never had enjoyed his few remaining years of life! And she would never have forgiven herself.

Her eyes closed tightly to hold back the threatening tears. But they began to force their way between her lashes and to flow down her cheeks. Twenty-one, she thought bleakly. What an age to die.

'Ohh!' she sobbed, rocking backwards and forwards in guilt and grief.

An arm stole around her and she gasped in shock, recoiling at the sudden appearance of the cause of her distress sitting beside her. Mercifully, he appeared to be dressed; a dark navy business suit filling her blurred vision.

'For God's sake! I'm comforting you,' Addan growled irritably, pulling her back into the shelter of his arms.

The soft, welcoming cloth impinged on her subconscious. 'I don't need your comfort!' she cried wildly, fighting for release.

He held her in a vice-like grip, scowling down at her, his face hard and determined. 'Calm down, Ellen!' he ordered gruffly.

'I don't need calming, I don't need comforting!' She sobbed helplessly, contrarily wanting to cry on his broad shoulder more than anything at this moment. For too long she'd been the strong one, running herself ragged for her dying husband. But wanting Addan's particular brand of comfort seemed like another betrayal.

'You do. You're crying——'

'I'm not!' she denied crossly.

His fingers slicked down the trail of salty tears,

skimming her cheekbones to the groove above her lip. 'What's this, then?' he asked drily.

'Sweat.'

'From your *eyes*?' he chuckled.

'The roof's leaking.'

'It's not raining. Why are you so stubborn? These are tears. . .' His thumb swept across her face. 'And these. . .'

'Get your hands off me!' she said jerkily, appalled to feel a warmth steal into her loins. How could she? 'Oh, Bruno!' she wailed.

'*Deus!*' Addan snatched away his hands as if she'd poured acid on them.

'Thank. . . God! Leave me. . .alone!' she moaned, burying her face in her hands.

She heard him rise and peeked out sullenly to see if he was going. He leant against the wall, his hands thrust into the pockets of his elegant jacket, his eyes dark and brooding.

'Not until I think you're in control of yourself,' he said harshly. 'You're in a mess. Are you on drugs or something?'

She glowered at him from beneath wet lashes and hugged her knees. 'Don't be ridiculous!'

'You hung around with an odd set,' he said shortly. 'It wouldn't surprise me. The last time I saw my brother alive he was drugged to the eyeballs. And you,' he scowled. 'You were red-eyed and wild. Taking heroin, were you?'

'No. Deep breaths,' she snapped irritably.

'Flippant bitch!' he growled.

She sighed, too overwrought to explain that she'd been desperately exhausted from Bruno's incessant demands. Poor darling. . .'I was upset,' she muttered resentfully. 'I'd been crying.'

'Because you weren't able to go skiing, or something, I suppose, after he'd woken up half-paralysed and the attention was on him for a change.'

Her eyes closed to shut him out and the horrifying

moment when they'd learned Bruno had a brain tumour. 'Vanish,' she said wearily, wishing she had a magic wand.

'Did I make you cry? Have I got under your thick skin at last?' he asked. Ellen gave him a scornful glare. 'OK. So I haven't. What is it, then? God!' He went chalk-white and clutched her arms fiercely. 'You're not pregnant?'

Ellen blinked. That was impossible. 'No, I'm not!'

Addan's breath exhaled noisily. 'What is it, then? Boyfriend trouble?' he hazarded, persisting. 'Is that why you've run from your friends in Paris?'

She tore herself away and jumped up, furious at his low opinion of her. 'You bastard! You think so little of me that when I cry you assume I must be grizzling over some trivial lover's tiff?' she raged.

'I've never seen you cry before.' Unperturbed by her outburst, he coldly held out a handkerchief, his eyes very watchful. 'Not even,' he added tightly, 'at Bruno's funeral.'

His hand was shaking imperceptibly. Her misty eyes flicked up but nothing in his bleak face suggested a reason. She wiped her eyes and face in the soft Egyptian cotton. For a long time she'd been just a zombie and zombies didn't cry.

'I had too many things to organise and cope with,' she said harshly, to keep back the destructive, useless self-pity. 'There wasn't time for tears.'

'Or you had none to shed.'

'I loved Bruno,' she declared defiantly. She had; maybe not as a wife, but as a sister, with affection and concern. . .'You've always refused to believe that ——'

'I know you didn't,' he muttered. 'You think I can't read body language?'

'What the devil is that supposed to mean?' she demanded nervously.

'My life has been spent watching people and their responses, reading the signs behind their words, beneath the lies, the deceits,' he said softly, his eyes a hard, piercing black. 'You treated Bruno with affection, like a brother. Not ever as a lover.'

Her stomach turned over. She stared at Addan in mute dismay. 'You're wrong,' she began hoarsely.

'I don't think so.' Addan stood up, looming over her.

She wanted to run but her whole body was turned to marble as if she'd been carved out of the floor. He took her face between his hands and studied it intently. Ellen tried to hold back her innermost secrets from his all-seeing eyes.

'This. . .is. . .intolerable!' she jerked out breathily.

'Look at me and tell me that you loved him with all the passion of a woman for a man!' he demanded through grated teeth.

She shut her eyes but his fingers dug into her flesh and she moaned, lifting her lashes in anguish. 'You have no right — '

'Say it!'

Ellen swayed, terrified by the crackling fury in every line of his face, the bared teeth, ready, it seemed, to tear at her flesh. His body steadied her and she trembled. 'I'm appalled — ' She began hoarsely.

'That I should face you with reality?' he said with brutal ruthlessness. His thumb began to rub her cheek with an indolent movement and Ellen was scared at the strength of her leaping pulses, looking up at Addan with unhappy eyes. 'I've seen couples in love, rare though that is, and you two weren't,' he growled. 'My parents loved one another deeply — to the extent that we were excluded from their lives. Perhaps that made Bruno desperate for flattery and vulnerable to it from the first female who showed interest.'

Her eyes became pained. 'Maybe he was astonished to meet someone who never once showed contempt for him!' she snapped. 'He idolised you! And you had nothing but scorn for everything he did!'

'It wasn't like that!' He frowned, sliding his palm absently up the side of her face. It was warm and strangely comforting and Ellen's instinct was to turn into it. 'Bruno needed directing. I felt a great responsibility towards him ——'

'You patronised him,' she said, jerking her head away from his knee-weakening caress. It wasn't fair that Addan should capture everyone so effortlessly, she thought grimly. 'You were always so much better at everything than he was. Bruno despaired of ever making you proud of anything he did.'

'Well, I certainly objected to him marrying merely to show me that he was mature enough to make choices,' Addan said curtly. 'My brother was obsessed by you because you were so beautiful. He believed that I'd be impressed by the kind of woman he could attract.'

'No,' she moaned, shaking her head emphatically, the shiny strands of her hair flicking his face. He was so close to the truth that she let out a wail of misery. 'Oh, please, Addan! Don't torment me like this!'

He reached out again and slid the swinging tresses behind each ear, a smouldering smile setting her heart thudding crazily. 'You deserve it — and more,' he said softly. 'With a relationship based on such a weak foundation, no wonder he was terrified of losing you and failing in the most important choice of all.'

'Stop, stop!' she croaked.

'So,' he continued relentlessly, 'he showered you with presents and let you have your own selfish way. And kept me strictly at arm's length, terrified even to tell me how ill he was because I might comfort you. And also because in that intimate situation,' he husked, 'he feared that we might be tempted to take that comfort a step further.'

'*No!*' she whispered, quivering like a leaf.

'But you were tempted, weren't you?' he murmured, his voice so soft that she found herself straining towards him to hear what he was saying. 'You wanted to surrender on both of the occasions when I kissed you,' he growled.

Her moist lashes fluttered helplessly in response to

the searing truth. She'd been tempted almost beyond endurance. 'I never ——'

'Not quite,' he agreed softly. 'But, hate me or not, you felt that primitive sexual attraction between us. And I think you only resisted because you didn't dare to risk offending Bruno. After all,' he murmured, 'as his wife, you became rich in your own right. That's far better than being any young or old man's darling, and you weren't going to jeopardise that kind of power and independence, were you?'

'I didn't marry him for his money!' she moaned.

'Of course you did!' Addan's tone hardened to steel. 'You were unemployed, your parents dead. Bruno was Santa Claus, Prince Charming and Croesus all rolled into one — with the advantage of being easily manipulated. And, knowing how cold you can be when something doesn't strike your fancy, I expect you never really gave your whole self to him sexually.'

Ellen gasped with indignation and shut her mouth quickly to hold back the impulsive words she longed to say. She couldn't betray Bruno again. If she tried hard, she could just keep her dignity and her bruised emotions till Addan left.

'My marriage is a closed book,' she said hoarsely, avoiding his hotly accusing eyes. 'What happened has absolutely no bearing on the fact that for you it's the end of your intrusion here. If you don't go, I'll throw caution to the winds and get the authorities round.'

He smiled. Nothing pleasant, just gloating menace. 'I think you'd better check your so-called rights over this house,' he suggested softly.

Startled, she met his eyes, not allowing herself to reveal the sudden clutch of sharp alarm that was cramping her stomach. 'Save me time. Tell me,' she demanded shakily. 'It's mine, isn't it?'

Addan folded his arms, a smug expression on his face. 'Not. . .entirely,' he murmured, watching her with unconcealed triumph.

# CHAPTER THREE

HE WAS bluffing. Ellen knew that. Yet. . .there was an air of terrible complacency about him that filled her with dread.

'Please. . .' On an impulse, she caught his arms, impatient to know why he looked so smug. 'Addan,' she said huskily, her eyes wide and pleading. 'Tell me what the problem is about this house. I have to know, you see, because I ——'

She gulped. His velvet eyes had softened and half closed, the fringe of lashes thick and dark. He was looking at her mouth speculatively, as if contemplating an assault on her gently parted lips. But she couldn't close them, because her breath was shallow in her chest and her body was charged with a heavy sexual tension that made every inhalation difficult.

When she dropped her bewildered gaze to his mouth, her heart began to pound at the message it was sending out. Miserably she saw that he intended to kiss her and she seemed quite incapable of stopping him, her limbs lethargic, her senses reeling.

His breath whispered over her lips, his dark head inclining downwards. She took a ragged breath and felt her eyes closing despite her desperate attempt to keep them open.

'Ellen,' he murmured in tones of intense longing.

'Addan!' she whispered, aware of the thudding urgency of her heart. There was a terrible hunger inside her for love, for comfort, making her frighteningly vulnerable. She swallowed and slowly lifted her lashes to look at him, meeting the slow simmer of his gaze with widening eyes.

Then, mercifully, his lips pressed together in a tight line. Carefully he lifted off her hands, a mocking expression on his face. 'I need a drink,' he said softly. 'How about you?'

Relief and disappointment hit her at the same time, muddling her totally. 'I—I don't know,' she mumbled. 'Yes. Yes—um—why not? I stopped off and bought some food——' distractedly she indicated the bags in the hall beside her Vuitton luggage '—but I can't remember if—um——'

Her hand lifted to push back her hair. What was she saying? Why didn't her mouth connect with her brain? She looked up at him, her eyes unhappy and shimmering.

Addan looked scornful. 'Practised little bitch, aren't you?' he drawled, and strolled towards the back of the hall.

Ellen glared and made an effort to concentrate. 'I wish I were! I'd lead you such a dance!'

He stopped dead. 'Would you?' he said in a flat tone.

'Over a cliff!' she answered irritably, and tried to pull herself together. 'Oh, don't worry, Addan. I don't have your malice. It's only wishful thinking. Show me the kettle and I'll find the tea and coffee. If you want wine,' she said curtly, 'you're out of luck. I didn't buy any.'

He looked over his shoulder at her in mild amusement. 'This is Madeira,' he said laconically. 'You're standing a few yards from one of the greatest vineyards on the island—and within drinking distance of one of the best *vinho generoso* in the world. Follow me.'

Feeling a little stupid, she obeyed, looking around the beautifully panelled hall with interest as they passed through it. For a house that had been abandoned for so long, it was in remarkably good condition. Perhaps it was something to do with the climate, she hazarded.

'Do you know if anyone's been keeping this place going while it's been empty?' she asked, catching him up as they entered the kitchen.

It was large—and bright, when Addan opened the shutters—and furnished with oak dressers and cupboards. Racks of Italian Blue Spode plates gave it a country air, though an enormous wicker basket of magnolia seedheads introduced an exotic note. She perked up, beginning to look forward to seeing the magnolias in bloom.

'The Quinta's upkeep should have been your responsibility — though that's a word I don't associate easily with you,' he said insolently.

She frowned. 'That's not my fault. I can't remember seeing any staff listed for the Quinta when I went through Bruno's holdings.'

He flinched. 'God!' he muttered. 'When he died, you must have thought it was your birthday! Thinking of you, counting up your assets, is deeply unpleasant. I understood that Bruno stopped paying the wages a while back — which you'd have noticed if you'd been really interested in the fine details of your acquisitions.'

She wished she'd persevered with trying to read all the documents that had littered her desk in a mind-boggling heap but it had been too much for her. Her dyslexia had let her down again. Left to her own devices, she could read tolerably well. Under stress, reading became almost impossible.

'What happened to the staff?' she asked anxiously.

He turned by the huge iron range, looking down his aristocratic nose in disapproval. 'The maid wrote to me saying she was worried about the house. The house, you notice, not her job. We Madeirans have a great sense of loyalty and a pride in our traditions. I put her on my payroll to keep the place ticking over — and the gardener. And,' he said, his voice tightening, 'the men who work the vineyard. Otherwise the whole place would have reverted to nature.'

'How awful!' she exclaimed, aghast. 'That would have been a crime. I wish I'd known ——'

'Spare me,' he drawled. 'Lots of things seem to have slipped your mind, or maybe you've conveniently never been told,' he said sarcastically, opening a cupboard and selecting two glasses. 'You really do have cotton wool between your ears, don't you? Don't you ever think further than the end of your prettily powdered nose? I suppose you're so used to sweeping into luxury hotels that it never occurs to you that someone actually keeps them operational. Places need cleaning, you know! I'm surprised you didn't go to Reid's Hotel and pick up another rich husband.'

She winced. 'Thank you for making sure the Quinta was maintained,' she said stiffly. 'I'm sorry I didn't know the maid was worried. If she'd written to Bruno or me——'

'I'm the one everybody relies on,' he said flatly. 'Not Bruno—and certainly not his merry widow. What were you expecting to do when you arrived here?' he said scathingly, waving the glasses carelessly in the air. 'Fight your way through the weeds and dust like some intrepid female explorer?'

'I didn't know and I didn't care what——'

His eyes blazed in the stark-boned face. 'You didn't care?' he repeated scornfully. 'My father's house was left to deteriorate, the vines to rot, and all because you and Bruno wanted to play around Europe like happy, truanting children!'

'I wasn't happy,' she yelled, deeply distressed by his low opinion of her. And that Bruno had neglected his family home.

'People who live purely for material gain never are,' Addan observed with cold pleasure. He tucked both glasses in one hand and abruptly turned to slam open the bolts on the French doors.

Ellen's shoulders drooped. Every time she gathered her strength a little, he slapped her down. And she couldn't take much more. Not one more word.

'I'm not like that, Addan,' she said wearily. 'I want to tell you all about it. I want you to listen to my side of it.'

Addan's spine stiffened. 'I don't want to think about the past any more. I'll never forgive you for whirling Bruno into a phoney life with even phonier people, when he had only a short time to live——'

'*He* wanted it, not me!' she yelled. And groaned. She'd promised. . .

Addan was turning, slowly, latent violence in the whole set of his body outlined against the glass doors. 'Bruno? Shy, antisocial, timid Bruno? Are we talking about the same man? The one I couldn't drag to dinner with friends, who never liked parties and certainly didn't like dancing?'

'He wanted to live every second he had left,' she said dully. No one would ever understand the situation.

'You're inventing that reason to absolve yourself from guilt about his death,' rasped Addan, his eyes merciless. 'But it won't wash. You began to burn candles at both ends the minute you got your hooks into him.' She stared at him dumbly. 'Explain that,' he said through his teeth. 'You were the dominant one. You did what you wanted, that was plain. And your submissive husband followed behind you like an obedient dog. How dare you insult his name by suggesting he forced you against your will to behave so stupidly? You've gone too far this time, Ellen!' he snarled, his face ravaged by fury. 'How dare you slur the name of Torre with such bald lies?'

'Forget I said it,' she muttered wearily, frightened by his fury. 'I'm sorry I did. Bitterly sorry.' She lifted miserable eyes to his, the suspicion of tears glimmering in them. 'Please,' she said brokenly. 'No more talk of the past, I beg you.'

'Crying again, Ellen?' he said through clenched teeth.

'Don't. . .don't torment me. I've had an awful time lately,' she admitted.

'You've —— ' He fell silent, watching her shrewdly.

His visible anger had come under control but it was like the calm centre of a storm. Ellen could see that he still simmered beneath his implacable exterior. His hands were in danger of snapping the stems of the tulip-shaped glasses he'd brought absently from his pocket. Seeing her gaze on them, he looked down, frowned and thoughtfully ran his fingers over the crest etched on each one as one would perhaps when making a vow, and the action chilled her to the marrow.

It was all or nothing, she told herself. He had to listen to reason. 'We both have had a bad time, you and I,' she said huskily. There was a flicker of a nervous pulse at the corner of his mouth and a shadowing of his dark eyes. He'd suffered. Of course he had, however much he might rant and rage. Encouraged, she took another risk. 'I understand how bad you must feel, not seeing Bruno for the six months before his death.'

'Do you?' he asked grimly. His jaw tightened but she knew it was in pain, not anger, his strong face suddenly looking quite desolate, and she felt his heartbreak as if it were her own. He'd loved his brother, and his self-imposed exile must have needed a will of iron.

'Oh, Addan,' she cried passionately, 'we all made mistakes! I should have acted differently too. I should have gone against Bruno's wishes and called you to say he was. . .near the end,' she whispered. 'But he was so insistent, so hysterical. . .' She dashed away a tear and tried to steady her croaky voice. 'I know we'll never be friends,' she said in a low tone, 'but I can't bear to think that we can't be civilised towards one another. Don't we owe it to Bruno?' Anxiously, her heart thudding frantically, she watched his reaction.

His head remained bent and for a few moments he toyed with the glasses, repeatedly tracing the etched design of the family crest. There was a tenseness in his jaw but she could tell that his brain was working overtime and she crossed her fingers hopefully.

' "Owe it to Bruno",' he repeated softly.

'Oh, yes!' she urged in desperation.

Slowly his head lifted. The dark, eloquent eyes were shuttered to Ellen's hopeful gaze, but his jaw seemed square and determined. Her heart thudded. There was something haggard about his expression, as if it racked him with pain to abandon his long-standing battle with her.

'For Bruno,' he mused, another battle obviously raging in his head. 'Maybe you weren't a spotless, virginal Snow White, nor the kind of woman I wanted my brother to marry,' he said, slowly, 'but I wasn't above reproach. I admit that. I've always regretted the pain I caused my brother because of you.' He frowned. 'It must have torn him apart when I arranged that he should be hounded by the police.'

'It did. He couldn't believe his own brother had turned him into a wanted man,' Ellen said gently. 'He thought it was a dreadful revenge.' She was in an agony of suspense. Addan had never owned up to making a mistake before. Maybe. . .

He heaved a deep, shuddering sigh and stared into space. 'Bruno suffered because of my. . .feelings towards you. I gave him a wedding night he'd never forget.' His shoulders rose with tension.

'Can you blame him for loving me?' she said passionately.

The dark lashes fluttered. 'No. Not at all. None of this was his fault. I absolved him from all responsibility long ago. I think I owe him something for what he had to endure. Yes,' he said softly and raised one empty glass. A shiver ran down Ellen's back at the unnatural glacial light flickering in Addan's stone-black eyes. 'I owe you, my brother,' he muttered almost inaudibly.

'You scare me!' whispered Ellen, shivering.

And to her amazement Addan smiled with a gentleness she hadn't seen before. 'I don't want you to be scared,' he said huskily.

'I thought —— '

'I know. I was angry. Bitter. That's all over now. I don't want you to be afraid of me ever again.'

She blinked, her face lifting to his in wide-eyed amazement. But she was still wary. You didn't trust a sleeping rattlesnake, she thought, trying not to raise her hopes too much. 'I'm not sure I ever was,' she said with some of her old defiance.

Addan laughed in genuine amusement. 'You are

quite something,' he said admiringly. 'A very powerful
lady.'

'There's not much point in keeping up our hostility
any longer, is there?' she said quietly.

His mouth tightened momentarily and then curved
into a dazzling smile. 'I have an idea. A pledge.' He
gave an awkward little chuckle as if he found his
concession to her rather difficult. 'Why don't we fill
these glasses with Madeira and drink a toast?'

'A toast?' she repeated doubtfully, hardly daring to
believe her ears.

'How else can we seal this matter once and for all?
You'd trust me if I pledged on my honour to remember
I owe something to my brother's wife, wouldn't you?'

'I suppose so,' she said slowly. That *seemed* all right.
She ventured a faint, hopeful smile.

'My word is my bond. You know that. You'll discover
I mean what I say in time. I'm glad you came, Ellen,' he
said astonishingly. 'It was a bit sticky at first, wasn't it?
But you're very persistent. Very persuasive.'

'I don't like bad feeling,' she said warily. 'I always
hated rows.'

'Of course. You were born to decorate the world, to
bring a little sparkle into people's lives, not to be
miserable,' he said, patronising her again. But this time
she let it go. 'I admire your strength of will in going for
what you want,' he continued in a gentle, persuasive
voice. 'Like water dripping on a stone, it's had some
effect. It's forced a decision on me.'

'Is that good or bad?' she asked wryly.

Amusement touched his hooded eyes for the first
time. 'Oh, good, very good,' he murmured. 'I feel
released from the past and finally set free.'

She allowed a hesitant smile to surface. 'Really?
You're not going to bare your teeth and snarl at me any
more?' she asked hopefully.

His own smile broadened. 'I'm only a wolf in sheep's
clothing,' he said.

Ellen tensed. 'I hope you didn't mean to say that.

The expression means that you're hiding your intentions under camouflage.'

'Oh. Do I mean a sheep in wolf's clothing, then?' he asked with worrying innocence and she wondered if she'd have to keep this particular wolf from the door still. 'You know what I mean. I'm definitely not going to fight you,' he said warmly, slipping the glasses into his jacket pocket again.

'I'm relieved to hear it.'

'You don't sound convinced. I don't blame you,' he sighed. 'But I can see my hostility has been a waste of time and energy. You have some admirable qualities and you deserve better.' His eyes glowed. 'I should have realised that a long while ago.' He took her faltering hand, kissed it and looked deep into her eyes. 'I pledge myself to your service.'

'Oh!' she cried, startled by his old-world gesture. 'Oh, Addan, if you really mean that, it's wonderful!' Suddenly, she too felt free, and the sensation was so new to her that she felt intoxicated already. Her eyes sparkled. On impulse, she stepped forwards and kissed him enthusiastically on both cheeks — and then hastily stepped back, blushing at her temerity. 'Don't read anything into that,' she warned solemnly.

'I won't,' he replied.

'Thank you.' The warm relief persisted. 'I can't tell you how glad I am we're not at loggerheads. I'm immensely happy,' she said blissfully, smiling back at him.

Her face felt as if it was suffused with joy and she wanted to throw her arms around him and hug him tightly. Her eyes darkened a little at the heavy drowsiness of his expression as if he was contemplating a meal. Of her.

'I'm glad.'

'This ——' Her lashes fluttered, worried that his eyes looked a little. . .*hungry*. She must be imagining it. 'This is something I've always longed for,' she said shyly, giving him the benefit of the doubt.

'Is it?' He let his hand touch her silken fall of hair and considered her parted lips thoughtfully. But his smile was innocent of cunning and totally beguiled her. 'How nice that you're getting what you've wanted,' he said easily. 'I know that you deserve it, for what you've done for my brother.'

She relaxed totally, the terrible past shed, the future an open book. It was something she'd wanted ever since she and Addan had first clashed. The sound of doves, cooing outside, seemed like a good omen to her, and she was unable to stop herself from beaming at him. 'It's wonderful to be really carefree again!'

His mouth twisted wryly. 'No responsibilities,' he sympathised.

Her eyes flipped upwards in mock-relief. 'Oh, those responsibilities!' she groaned.

'Poor Ellen.' He kissed her forehead, his lips cool. 'You're not really cut out for hard work, are you?'

'I —— ' She was about to protest, but decided not to start another argument. Maybe later, when she could fully trust him, she'd talk to him, particularly about the last year, and he'd respect her more. 'I *am* here on holiday,' she smiled.

'Then we'll start it properly. Come on, let's go outside. The evening's warm, the garden inviting.' With an extravagant gesture, he flung open the tall French doors.

The view melted any lingering apprehension clean away. It was the first time she'd seen the back of the house. When she'd arrived, she'd dumped her cases in the hall and dashed upstairs with her beauty box and overnight bag. Seeing Addan in bed had put her immediate plans clean out of her mind.

'Oh, it's just wonderful!' she cried in delight, moving forwards and stopping, entranced.

'One of the most spectacular *quintas* on the island,' he said in a murmur that caressed the air and spoke of his deep love for his home.

She nodded, her eyes glistening with a quiet delight.

When she'd arrived, she'd thought the imposing front gardens had been beautiful enough — dropping to a valley and then rising again to hills and high mountain peaks — but this part of the extensive grounds was even lovelier.

'The sea,' she cried excitedly. 'There's a view of the sea.' A panorama, in fact, sweeping down from the plateau where they stood, in a series of intensively cultivated green terraces towards the glinting sapphire Atlantic. 'How blue it is!' she said in awe.

Addan followed her gaze. 'It's very, very deep,' he said quietly. 'Madeira is surrounded by some of the deepest seas in the world. I really had forgotten how very lovely it was.' He scanned the billiard-table lawns, backed by a group of exotic palm trees. 'And some Crown of Henry are out,' he said softly to himself, eyeing some clumps of vivid blue agapanthus, whose colour rivalled that of the sea.

'Crown of Henry!' she repeated smiling broadly. 'Is that in honour of Henry the Navigator?'

'You do know some history,' he said in surprise.

Ellen grinned. 'Odd to think that the island was deserted when that Zarco guy discovered it. Unless you believe the legend about that other guy who was shipwrecked just off the east coast.'

'Robert Machin, the Englishman? It's possible,' he acknowledged.

'He ran off with his mistress,' she said, her eyes wistful. 'People were against their marriage too. I feel great sympathy for him and the woman he loved. It's awful being hounded, Addan.'

'I realise that,' he said huskily, standing negligently against the gnarled trunk of a huge wistaria.

'Machin and his mistress must have sighted land and been overjoyed,' she sighed. 'How tragic that their ship was wrecked! I think of them, swimming for the shore and dying in each other's arms,' she said, her romantic soul touched by the story.

'Very poignant,' he agreed. 'Doubly so. It's always

terrible, isn't it, to have your hopes raised by thinking you're home and dry, only to have them dashed again by a spiteful fate?'

There was an odd timbre to his voice, and she slanted her eyes at him to identify the reason, but he grinned cheerfully at her and she decided that she'd been mistaken.

She put the past away and sighed in contentment for the delights of the present. Her gaze took in the richly planted garden; the hibiscus, roses, exotic orchids. . . Lifting her nose to the air, she sniffed extravagantly, scenting a medley of perfumes on the gentle evening breeze.

'Half my house-plants are growing here — at twenty times the size! I can hardly believe this. It's. . .' She was speechless. It didn't need words — and they'd be inadequate, anyway.

Thrilled to the core that this place belonged to her, she leant dreamily against the whitewashed wall beneath a long veranda covered in the delicate fronds of a gnarled wistaria. In blissful silence, she let her surroundings soothe her agitated mind completely. How wonderful. To spend the rest of her life here, safe, secure, wrapped in such beauty. Shafts of mellow evening sun touched her radiant face, imbuing it with a rich, warm gold.

'It's what? Valuable? A splendid piece of real estate?' prompted Addan encouragingly.

She smiled, her lips parting softly. What a materialist he was! That came of thinking about nothing but endless profit margins. 'The most beautiful place I've ever seen,' she said huskily. 'If only I knew some poetry! I might be able to describe a place like this that simply takes your breath away.'

He nodded. 'People would pay a good deal for this estate. Although it has some drawbacks — it's not everyone's cup of tea. Islands can seem enchanting, but this particular site is very remote, of course. Nothing, I'm afraid, but plants, views, silence.'

She nodded contentedly, admiring the huge red poinsettias encircling a tall stone figure of Adonis. Isolation was just what she'd wanted. Everything else was a bonus. And when Addan had gone, she'd have it all to herself! An incandescent smile curved her full mouth and she heaved a satisfied sigh.

'I've never been anywhere without the intrusion of civilisation,' she said quietly. 'Noise, crime, traffic, crowds or pollution. . .sometimes all of those. Even on the ski slopes we were surrounded by boisterous friends. I can't believe Bruno and I were married for four years and yet we never came here.'

'I expect he knew it wouldn't suit you,' said Addan casually. 'The Quinta isn't your kind of place. No fax machines, no smart set next door to have round to dinner, no glittering, chattering classes to discuss the latest books—oh,' he said quickly. 'Bruno told me you didn't read much.'

Ellen tensed. Did Addan know she was dyslexic? That reading was an infinite labour? No, she decided, he looked faintly scornful, as if he imagined she found reading a bore rather than a chore. She relaxed a little. 'Not a crime, is it?' she asked lightly, carefully guarding her secrets.

'A shame.' He studied her for a few moments. 'There's more to life than flicking through glossy magazines.'

She winced, remembering his caustic comment of long ago, when he'd seen her doing just that and asked her if it was worthwhile buying magazines just for the fashion pages. 'Don't ruin a beautiful view,' she muttered.

He gave her a lop-sided grin. 'My apologies. That was unforgivable.' Ellen looked at him in surprise and he smiled disarmingly. 'It's something of a novelty, being nice to you,' he told her solemnly.

'I know. I'm finding it odd,' she admitted. 'I expect you to turn on me and take a bite,' she said ruefully, and they laughed together. 'Oh,' she sighed dreamily.

'I'm sure we're finding it hard to be hostile to one another because it's so tranquil here.'

'You really do appreciate the beauty of the Quinta, don't you?' he mused.

An intuitive caution made her choose her words carefully. She looked away from him to the orange-roofed houses, scattered like confetti on the intensively cultivated terraces that ran down to the coast, far below. She mustn't seem too keen. He wasn't to be trusted with any information about herself at all — she'd always instinctively known that. Given a chance, he'd spoil her plans.

'It's a lovely setting. Islands are exciting. I'm told the climate's good, the scenery is dramatic and it's a botanist's paradise. Bruno called it a floating garden. But as you say — ' she smiled, mischievously trying to look like a social butterfly. If that was what his fixed mind had decided, then she'd give it to him, she decided ' — the Quinta is some way from a decent shopping arcade. Fancy having to drive into Funchal every time you want designer clothes!'

'Fancy.' He seemed to relax. 'A dire place to be alone, too!' he laughed.

She cocked her head on one side and grinned as if in agreement. By being stupid, she was no threat to him. Her ploy was working! In another half-hour or so, he'd get tired of hanging around a simpering airhead and disappear.

'I can imagine! Deadly dull. Lead me to the wine,' she suggested. 'It's *ages* since I had a drink.'

She could see him registering the fact that his sister-in-law probably used alcohol as a crutch for her 'empty, shallow life'. Amused by her deception of such a perceptive man, she demurely walked along a path carpeted in tiny cream stars, the richly scented blossom from a shady tree. Bees hummed in a soothing drone and she stopped in pleasure, a great swelling in her heart.

'Something wrong?' murmured Addan.

'No. . .no. . .' She couldn't tell him. Nothing could describe how she felt. Yet something about the setting filled her with awe. There was a quality of serenity and timelessness about her surroundings, a sense of being embraced and welcomed into an old and friendly culture. She felt totally at home after years of restlessly seeking happiness.

And it had been here, waiting for her, all the time.

If only she'd known! Tears glimmered in her eyes. 'Hayfever, I think,' she said hastily, explaining to the astonished Addan. 'My body's used to cities.'

He grunted, accepting her explanation, and reached behind a clump of papyrus, bringing out an enormous iron key from the wall of an outbuilding. 'This is the *loja do vinho*,' he said, as the key grated in the lock. 'A wine storehouse.'

'I thought you had to keep wine in cellars?' she said curiously, stepping in and looking around at the huge goatskins hanging from the rafters and the stacks of enormous wicker baskets.

'That's France,' he answered dismissively. 'You know the story of "come-back wine" — *vinho da roda*?'

Intrigued, she crossed the earthen floor where he was searching along racks, where the bottles were stored. 'No. I must have missed that. Heavens, Addan! Shouldn't the bottles be on their sides, so that the corks are covered?'

He shook his head, a half-smile playing about his mouth. 'Not a practice we follow. Our wine's powerful enough to crumble the corks,' he said quietly.

'Oh!' She looked doubtfully at the ancient bottle in his hand. 'In that case, I'm not sure I want any! It could play havoc with my stomach lining.'

'Chemical reactions don't work that way,' he said in amusement. 'Just because one substance has a strong reaction to another, it doesn't mean others do. Often they remain inert. That's one of the mysteries of life.'

'Like us,' she said wryly. 'We exploded like dynamite the minute we met.' He nodded, clearly amused by the comparison. 'That was an experiment I wouldn't want to repeat. Who's to say my stomach won't react alarmingly to your wine if it's that powerful?' she asked uncertainly.

'Because it's evolved from centuries of growing practices,' he said laconically, resting the bottle on a huge cask. He eyed her with twinkling black eyes. 'What we have here is something that has matured to perfection.' Ellen looked at him solemnly. Was he talking about the wine or himself? His mocking mouth twitched appealingly at the corners. 'It's not some young, thin-bodied vintage that turns sour in time,' he said smoothly. 'It improves with age. The minute it touches your lips, you'll know what it will do to your insides.'

'You're a good salesman, I'll say that for you,' she said with a small laugh. A drink would be a good idea. It would occupy both of them, give her a diversion. She had to do something to take her mind off his sinfully seductive mouth.

'I don't need to talk. The wine will do it for me,' he grinned. 'And believe me, this vintage has qualities that will stagger you. Rich, warming, intoxicating. Quite irresistible.'

'Intoxicating.' She frowned, still doubtful about what they were doing.

'You're not going to insult me by refusing my wine, are you? Now I would have put you down as a woman who'd try anything once,' he said unfairly. 'Not scared of tasting the results of years of perfecting the Torre skills, are you?'

'Of course not.' There was, she thought ruefully, something about Addan's approach to wine that echoed his feelings about women. Trying each one and moving on to another.

'Let's sample the barrels, then, and select whichever variety you like best,' he said with satisfaction, replacing the bottle on the shelf. 'I'd like you to think that you've had a hand in making your choice.' His eyes danced with mysterious lights. 'Then we'll sit on the terrace and watch the sun go down and I'll tell you about "come-back wine".'

'Sounds lovely,' she said cautiously, wondering how soon she could ask him to leave.

'I'll do my best to make it so.'

His voice was a little too sultry, a fraction too throbbing. Ellen felt her nerves tightening again and she wondered what he really was doing here — and, even more important, what he intended to do. A faint frown troubled her face. It looked as if she'd find out very soon.

# CHAPTER FOUR

ADDAN shifted his weight and she flinched. He looked at her curiously but made no comment on the paleness of her apprehensive face. 'These are a few kept back for the cellars,' he said casually, rapping on the oak cask and listening to the sound. 'Most of the wine is rather unromantically produced in purpose-built buildings on the estate. I think these have been maturing for just two years now.'

'Two years!' she repeated in surprise, steadying her irrationally jumping nerves. She didn't have to be worried about him. They'd made a pact.

He took a silver tube from a lidded wicker basket and looked up at her briefly from under his lashes. 'You must learn about our wine. It goes through a complicated process over a period of time.'

He dipped the tube into the cask, bringing it out filled to the brim. His hand was totally steady as he poured out a glorious golden liquid into one of the tulip glasses and handed it to her.

'This is Sercial,' he said in loving tones. 'The driest Madeira. It comes from vineyards two thousand feet up in the mountains. Hold the glass to the light. What colour is it?'

'Pale gold,' she suggested. 'Around. . .nine carat?'

Addan laughed. 'Nice analogy. Now inhale the bouquet.'

She put her nose to the narrow glass and sniffed. 'I can hardly——'

Addan's hand enclosed hers and she looked up, startled, a little alarmed, her huge eyes as wary as a deer's. 'Swirl,' he commanded. 'It intensifies the bouquet.'

And my nerve-endings, she thought anxiously. Was

he doing this deliberately? As part of his eternal need to seduce any female under eighty? 'I only wanted to have a drink,' she protested. 'Do I have to go through all these preliminaries?'

'Far too simple! Don't you believe in foreplay?' he asked lazily. 'Surely you of all people know that it intensifies the experience!'

Ellen frowned at him. 'Foreplay with wine?' she asked, askance.

'Why not? Please. Sip. Roll the liquid around the mouth. That's right. Think with your senses. Tell me what you taste, what you. . .' His voice flowed warmly, as rich as old brandy and she felt her hand tremble in his. 'Tell me what you feel, deep down inside. Use your instincts rather than say what you think you should.'

She blinked and then lowered her eyes in confusion, taking refuge in assessing the wine and trying to behave as if her senses weren't reeling drunkenly already. To her irritation, he kept his hand on hers and guided the glass to her lips, watching intently as she sipped.

'Oh, it's delicious!' she exclaimed. Her eyes held his a moment too long. She ran the tip of her tongue over her jutting lower lip and stopped quickly when his eyes darkened hungrily.

'Sure it is,' he said quietly. 'If it was good enough for Michelangelo, it's good enough for you.'

'Good heavens! What a thought! I want to try another one,' she said, the briskness she'd intended sounding rather shaky when she registered how carnal his mouth had become.

'I'm pleased you're so eager. Verdelho,' he drawled, filling her glass again, caressing the word. 'This is also an aperitif. Something to tantalise the taste-buds, to whet the appetite.'

She looked at him suspiciously but he merely smiled with a friendly innocence. But he'd come very close to her, the rise and fall of his chest an inch or so away, his attentive face bending to hers like a lover's. Small quivers of arousal chased over her skin where his breath stirred the small hairs of her face.

If I didn't know better, she thought apprehensively, I would have said he was trying to seduce me again.

Her suddenly serious blue eyes lifted to his. He raised a querying eyebrow. She felt nothing but tension between them, drawing her to him like an invisible and undeniable force. Darkly velvet, his eyes melted into hers and her lips parted in a high, arching bow, traitorously demanding his kiss.

His head angled and she found that her limbs were refusing to move and he would almost certainly think she was willing.

The terrible thing was that she almost hoped he would.

Fortunately for her self-respect, he didn't. 'What do you think of this one?' he asked quietly.

Blinking, she saw he held the glass out to her and she flashed him an unconvincing smile, her heart pumping so fast that her hand slopped some of the liquid. His long fingers closed around the slender stem of the glass and his head bent to her hand before she knew what he was doing. And he caught the drops on his tongue, the soft warmth of it sliding on her skin, making her gasp.

'Addan! Really — !'

'Can't waste it,' he argued, sounding far more normal than she did. 'How do you rate this colour?' he asked in perfectly calm tones.

'What? I — oh!' Ellen focused on the glass. The colour. *Think!* she scolded herself. 'Eighteen carat,' she pronounced eventually.

'Very good.'

Ellen didn't look at him. That approval could have been for rapidly recovering from near-danger, not for assessing his wine. Obediently she did the swirling, the sniffing, made the right kind of noises and took a sip, thankful that he wasn't touching her any longer.

'Not so dry as the last one.' Remembering the wine buffs on television, she slanted her eyes at him, intending to lift the tension a little. 'I get nuts,' she said brightly.

He grinned and she knew from the gleam in his eyes that he was aware of her deliberate attempt to lighten the sultry atmosphere. 'What kind of nuts?'

'Peanuts.'

Addan's grin broadened. 'And I've got a nasty idea you're teasing me,' he complained ruefully. 'Be careful, Ellen. I can tease, too. It makes life more fun, doesn't it? I can't wait to get to the climax.'

'I beg your pardon?' she said stiffly, her perkiness vanishing in an instant.

'Oh, dear, oh, dear, Ellen,' he chided, wagging his finger at her. 'Can't you think of anything but sex? I'm talking about the moment when we settle down to indulge ourselves in your final choice. But we have a little way to go yet. Try this one. . .'

He spoke very quietly, as if there was an intimacy between them. She tore her eyes from his compelling face and fixed them on the silver dipper. Ellen noticed a little dazedly how long his fingers were, and that they had been impeccably manicured. She remembered how his hands had once explored her embarrassingly yearning body with firm assurance and yet a delicate, tantalising touch.

'I still think we could have grabbed a bottle and be sitting in the sunshine by now,' she muttered, emptying the last of the wine. A few drops spilled on to her chin.

'Not again!' he marvelled. 'How shaky your hand is!' He reached out and his index finger was sweeping away the droplets. And then his mouth was there too. Briefly. When he drew back, there was no expression on his face at all and hot, burning fires in her chest. 'Do I make you nervous or is it something else?' he enquired solicitously.

'You're rushing me,' she complained.

'I thought I was going rather slowly,' he said with a bland smile. 'Anyway, we've finished with the appetisers now. Time for the more powerful wines.' He steadied her hand. 'Sweeter, darker.' Ellen tried not to look at his sensual lips. 'More intense, more body, you understand.'

Perhaps she was weak from the wine; she didn't know. Only that when he lifted her hand and guided it to his own lips, sipping from her replenished glass, she felt an overwhelming urge to reach up and taste the flavour of the wine on his moistened mouth.

'How—how many more types are there?' she asked falteringly. 'I'll be under the table if I drink much more.'

'We're almost finished. One more. Surely you're used to drinking?' he murmured. 'Try the last one. Malvásia. Malmsey—the stuff chosen by the Duke of Buckingham to be drowned in. A wonderful way to go, don't you think?'

Her laughter eased the tense anticipation inside her. 'It gives a whole new meaning to the phrase 'dead drunk', doesn't it?' she giggled, and was ridiculously pleased when Addan roared with laughter, throwing his head back and dazzling her with his perfect white teeth.

'I wouldn't want you drunk.'

Her eyes flicked up warily. That was an ambiguous statement if she'd ever heard one! 'Neither would I,' she said wryly, taking his remark at face value. Cautiously she savoured the sweet, mellow liquid. 'But it's gorgeous!' she cried in surprise.

'OK. Which are we to take outside to drink?'

'The second one,' she said quickly, not choosing her favourite. 'The last two are a little too rich and powerful for me.'

'Is there such a thing as *too* rich and powerful, do you think?' he mused, looking directly at her.

'You know there is,' she answered steadily. 'Too much of a good thing——'

'Can take you to the extreme limits of human pleasure,' he suggested smoothly.

'Or a Black Hole,' she said ruefully and he laughed again.

'That journey's off. I'm taking you on another trip instead. Nearer to home.' He saw her wary frown and shook his head sorrowfully. 'Discovery,' he chided, waving an arm at the stored wines.

'I don't mind exploring,' she said wryly, 'providing I don't get shipwrecked at the end.'

Addan regarded her steadily. 'This is a wine-tasting, not a voyage into the unknown. I don't know about you, but I know exactly where I'm going.'

She flushed at his light reprimand and vowed to keep her doubts about his intentions to herself. 'So do I,' she said firmly. 'And you said I could choose the wine. So let's have the one that won't make my head spin like a top.'

'As you insist. It's an interesting choice, though. A mirror of life, maybe? Are you afraid of losing control?' he asked softly.

'I'm interested in self-preservation,' she answered drily. 'Don't you think I'd be a fool to choose something so rich and powerful that it could turn my head? I've had a small taste of what you have to offer me. I'll stick at that, thanks.'

'But you did like it,' he persisted gently.

Ellen began to feel confused. She wasn't sure what she or Addan were talking about — Madeira wine or his intoxicating kisses, the enticing smell that emanated from his pores, the gorgeous warm smoothness of his skin. . .

'I like cream buns and chocolate cake,' she said. 'But they're not good for me and I know when I've had enough.'

'Madeira wine won't harm you. It's taken for pleasure and a tonic as well,' he said, apparently amused by her fending. 'It's claimed to revive and stimulate the body, filling it with vitality and power.'

'Sounds like the elixir of life,' she said brightly.

His mouth quirking, he carefully selected a bottle from the shelf, his hands brushing off the dust, smoothing over the curves of the bottle in an almost sensual movement. Ellen gulped, her treacherous pulses leaping erratically.

'Let's go and find out, shall we? Personally, I prefer something full-bodied,' he said, wickedly slanting laughing eyes at her. 'But then, that's how I like my women: a bit of bite, a fullness in the mouth ——'

She licked her lips, appalled at how easily he scattered her senses with his sinful talk. Anxious to get out, she walked straight into a skein of spiders' webs, and struck out at them in alarm. Her arms were suddenly pinned to her sides and she was being hauled backwards, her spine fitting all too well into Addan's firm body.

'What ——?' she gasped.

'Superstition,' he drawled in her ear. Warmth and the sweet fragrance of wine on his breath skimmed across her face tantalisingly.

Ellen tried to escape the iron band of his arm, wrapped firmly around her waist. 'Super what?' she asked in confusion.

'You must never touch cobwebs,' he said gently, lifting thick white strands from her hair. 'I had to stop you quickly. Sorry if I alarmed you, but it's an old tradition that clearing cobwebs means clearing away good fortune.' His tone became softer. 'I feel my fortunes have improved dramatically in the last half-hour and I wouldn't want you to sweep away my luck.'

Bewildered, she felt his hand shift and Ellen watched its progress wide-eyed, mesmerised by its slow, inexorable movement upwards. 'Addan,' she said hoarsely, her breasts rising and falling with her rapid breathing. 'I'm ——'

'Mmm?' He nuzzled her neck contentedly.

She quivered and sucked in her breath, pressing back into his body to escape the roaming fingers which were creeping nearer and nearer to the high swell of her breast. 'Ohh!'

He'd spun her around with effortless skill, drawn her to him and was contemplating an assault on her mouth.

Before she could stop him, he placed a hand behind her head, gathering her hungrily to him. Their lips met in a fusing of flames, both of them devouring each other, the kisses from one hotly inciting the other.

Ellen moaned huskily in her throat as Addan's plundering lips began to ravish every inch of her face, his unleashed passion firing a raging need inside her.

'Ellen, Ellen,' he breathed, bending her pliant body till she was forced to cling to his shoulders for balance. She whimpered in an attempt to protest, but her weak body was revelling in his adoration and refused to co-operate.

In the glorious garden, she seemed a part of nature, following her instincts. And this was right, she thought hazily, as Addan's lips returned to savour every inch of her mouth. It felt right, he smelt gorgeous, tasted. . .a shudder ran through her from top to toe as the tip of his tongue gently edged along her arched, pouting mouth.

He tasted so good she wanted more. 'More,' she mumbled, unaware that she'd spoken.

The effect on Addan was electrifying. 'God, Ellen!' he said hoarsely, pushing her away. 'Tempt the devil, not me!'

Her huge eyes were drowsy and slightly glazed. 'What?' she said, before she could recover herself.

He kissed her forehead chastely. 'Nothing,' he said softly. 'I apologise.'

'You. . .apologise?' she repeated stupidly, playing for time so that she could slow down her galloping heartbeat and fight her way from the ridiculous trance his kisses seemed to have placed on her.

'Yes. Sorry,' he said, his face very serious. A bewildered expression came to his face. 'I don't know what happened to me. Perhaps. . .no. That's crazy. . .'

'What is?' she encouraged warily, consumed with curiosity to know what was making the decisive Addan look as if he'd been socked between the eyes.

He shrugged, apparently irritated with himself. 'The fact that for some reason I feel elated and felt an

impulse — hell, don't look at me like that!' he pleaded.
'It was innocent enough. I suddenly felt very, very
happy.' He frowned. 'I'm not sure why.'

'Happy.' Steadier now, her pulses were only canter-
ing along like the winner of the Derby.

Addan took her trembling hands and kissed them
like a brother and all the time she was wishing he'd take
her trembling body and kiss it like a lover. Oh, darn it!
she groaned inwardly. *Why* did she find this man so
utterly irresistible?

'My sweet Ellen,' he sighed, 'here I go again. But I
think I had to kiss you, I have to touch you.'

'Well, thanks,' she said with some asperity. 'I'm not
sure if I'm annoyed with you or insulted.'

'It was, you see,' he said in a companionable way, 'a
catharsis.'

He tucked her arm in his and patted her hand as if
they were a couple of pensioners going on a stroll and,
contrarily, she didn't want that kind of response from
him at all. Now it's Darby and Joan, she thought, her
mind spinning like a crazy top.

'You mean you've got rid of all your old aggression
by crushing me to your manly bosom in a gesture of
warmth and friendship?' she suggested lightly.

'That's it! Women are awfully good at this sort of
thing, aren't they?' he sighed. 'It baffles me, this
emotion stuff. But now we've touched, had an affectionate little hug, and broken the ice, I hope we can put
all the past behind us, Ellen. I'd like us to spend the
next few days in relative — relative —' he laughed,
amused by his own joke ' — harmony.'

'The next few days.' Ellen frowned. She sounded like
a parrot, but there was something blocking her mind:
pure physical need. No one had ever relieved that; only
Addan had constantly aroused it and failed to satisfy it
and now she felt as if her body would burst with the
ungovernable burning inside her.

He gallantly brushed the seat of a white-painted cast-
iron seat, handed her on to it and excused himself while

he went back for the wine. In a daze, she sat and listened to the liquid birdsong filling the evening air with clear, pure notes that made her want to cry and laugh all at the same time. Oh, heavens! Her emotions were in a turmoil! she thought ruefully.

'You have forgiven me, haven't you? It won't happen again,' he reassured her, pouring the drinks. 'I've got it out of my system.'

'Good,' she said faintly, wishing she had.

'If I upset you, then I'm terribly sorry. But I think it's been something of a watershed for both of us, hasn't it?'

'It has?'

'Ellen!' he reproached gently. 'It was your idea.'

'What was?' she frowned, losing the thread. She had the impression that he was spinning a web for her and she'd just been caught. The spider wasn't bringing *her* much luck.

'It was your idea to forget our differences for Bruno's sake. I began by doing that for my brother first and now I'm doing it for me — because I feel such a sense of relief to be taking some positive action,' he said smoothly. 'I can't honestly say I'm being friendly for *your* sake yet, because it's early days,' he told her with remarkable candour. 'But I'm sure that by the time we both leave the island there'll be a change in the way we think of each other.'

His voice was warm and golden, like the sun that seeped into her. But the sun was setting, and she couldn't get it out of her mind that Addan's conversation just didn't ring true.

'It's a nice thought,' she said non-committally.

'To the beauties of Madeira,' he said, raising his glass. 'I hope you have time to explore a little, before you leave.'

'I'm —' A guardian angel stopped her from confiding in him. 'I'm not sure,' she said, instead of telling him that she wasn't leaving at all. 'What about you? Staying long?' she asked as casually as she could.

'Just a few days, till I've completed some business,' he smiled.

'You have business here? Surely Bruno inherited your parents' interests in Madeira and Portugal?' she said suspiciously. 'You took over the Brazilian end, didn't you?'

'I did,' he agreed, idly watching a butterfly sitting on the edge of her glass. 'What a life that creature has,' he mused.

'Short,' she pointed out wryly.

'And sweet. Days of sipping nectar, oblivious of the future.'

'Your business here,' she prompted, not liking his obvious comparison with her.

'Yes. I have friends here of long standing.' He dazzled her with a beaming smile and she thought of the blonde, a small tinge of annoyance ruffling her composure. 'There's also an important deal I want to clinch. Nothing I can't handle in a day or so,' he murmured.

'Oh.' She'd hoped he'd fly back to Rio at the earliest opportunity. Sharing the house with the man whose touch she hungered for like a lovesick pop-groupie would be difficult. 'The house,' she reminded him sweetly. 'You hinted that you had a right to entry. You were kidding, weren't you?'

'Not in the least,' he drawled. 'The situation is quite clear in the deeds.'

'I. . .haven't looked at them.' She frowned anxiously.

'I thought not. I'll give you some advice,' he said, his hand resting on her knee in a friendly fashion. 'I know you're not keen on reading, but whenever you're confronted with a document of any kind do try to go through it. Thoroughly. Especially the small print.'

Ellen remained silent. The last year had been nothing but reading; documents, demands, summonses. . . The words had jumped around in their usual way, never staying still long enough for her to understand what they meant without a great deal of effort. The paperwork had been very hard for her to cope with. No wonder she was mentally exhausted.

In any case, her solicitor had explained everything to her — though she'd been in such a state of shock that she hadn't listened with her whole-hearted attention. His voice had droned on and on, he'd asked repeatedly if she followed everything and she'd mumbled that she had. But there was only one thing that she really understood — that she was facing an unparalleled muddle. What he'd told her about Bruno's financial situation had devastated her on top of the recent trauma of Bruno's death.

'I'll try,' she said, forcing the submissive words out.

'The fact is,' Addan continued casually, sipping his drink, 'there's nothing really dramatic to reveal. Only that Bruno and I — now you and I, of course — share the contents of the cellar. I'm allowed reasonable access to purloin whatever bottles I want, on a civilised agreement with the owner. That's you,' he said cheerfully.

She forced a smile. 'In that case, we'd better have a sort-out this evening and divide everything up straight away.'

'No rush, is there?' he said lazily. 'Or are you making a quick sale of the property before you dive back to the high life?'

'I think that in the circumstances we ought to know who owns what,' she said, not answering his sly question. 'Let's get things divided up. If there are any pictures or personal items in the house you want, you'd better list them and I can get them crated up for you.'

'Generous,' he murmured appreciatively. 'Officially the contents belong to you. There are some things I want here, however, and I'd like to stake my claim as soon as possible.'

Ellen felt relieved that he'd be out of her hair soon, with nothing in the Quinta to bring him back ever again. 'We can settle this up amicably, I'm sure,' she said, feeling she could afford to be warm and friendly now. 'We'll both know where we stand. You can get on with your life and I with mine.'

'Those are my sentiments exactly,' he said huskily. 'It'll be very satisfying to clear away the debris of the past. And gratifying to have the things I've wanted to possess for some time and haven't been able to. I'm eager to get my hands on them, I must admit.'

He was smiling at her with apparent sincerity, but still something in his tone, his shadowed eyes, made her shiver. Intuitively, she felt he was up to no good, but she wanted to trust him because she couldn't bear the thought of facing Addan's hostility any longer.

'Fine,' she said firmly. 'We'll go through the house systematically and then the wine store. Then you can see your friends, do your business and book your flight home, knowing everything's properly dealt with.'

'Wonderful!' he approved. 'You're quite efficient really, aren't you, under that butterfly exterior?'

'Oh, I wouldn't say that,' she demurred as prettily as she could, fluttering her lashes ridiculously.

Addan laughed at her teasing. 'Seriously, I'm grateful to you for letting me stay a day or so. It's important to me.' He took her hands. 'You see, Ellen,' he said quietly, 'I need to work through the memories I have of this house. Since you're selling——'

'Does the idea upset you?' she asked curiously.

He let her go and turned away, looking towards the rosy sky in the west. 'My close links were severed some time ago,' he said evenly. There had been no tremor of longing in his voice, but his thigh muscles were tensed, stretching the fine fabric of his suit. 'After all, I have a home in Rio. Lovely place. But I'd like to exorcise a few ghosts. Say goodbye. You understand?'

'I know how important it is to say goodbye to things you love,' she said quietly. 'My parents died when I was fourteen.'

'I didn't know. I know little about you other than what Bruno told me. Of what?' he asked huskily.

'An accident. Father was moonlighting, driving lorries, and Mother went with him. He was tired from holding down two jobs and getting little sleep and simply drove off the edge of the motorway.'

'I'm sorry,' Addan said gently.

She nodded. 'So you see, I understand what it's like to lose your parents,' she mumbled. 'It was so sudden, no warning. . . My well-meaning aunt wouldn't let me see them, even though I begged her. I suppose —— ' She choked back a sob and his hands clasped hers in understanding.

'I expect your aunt wanted you to remember them as they were,' he said in a low tone.

'I know, but I always had a sense of something unfinished.' Addan was very still and she suddenly realised this must be painful for him too. 'Forgive me,' she said gently. 'I've brought back memories for you. Were you able to say goodbye?'

'Yes and no,' he answered, his eyes downcast. 'I said the words to them but I don't think I grieved. I knew I had to be very adult, you see. Everyone seemed to be looking to me, wondering what I'd do. What happened to you — did your aunt look after you?'

'Not very enthusiastically,' Ellen sighed. 'She was rather appalled to be landed with me. I don't blame her; she was used to uncomplicated sons. A fourteen-year-old girl can be difficult.' She'd lost all the love she'd ever had, she thought sadly, remembering how much she'd cried — till her aunt had lost patience.

'So you went to Amsterdam as soon as you could.'

'I ran away, actually.'

'That takes some courage,' he commented shrewdly.

She toyed with her glass. 'It did, yes,' she confessed. 'I chose the flattest country I could think of — I don't like heights, you see — and took off into the blue. Freedom had mixed blessings. I was very lonely. And hungry,' she said ruefully.

'Creature of impulse. Perhaps you should have waited till you had qualifications and could get a decent job.'

Ellen sensed a slight reproof in the murmured words and decided to let him continue thinking she was stupid. Academically, she thought morosely, she supposed she was.

'My work went to pot when my parents died and I had to move schools. I couldn't concentrate and lost such a lot of ground that I don't think I could ever catch up.' She smiled. 'I knew for a long time that I'd have to exist on my wits.'

Addan's eyes narrowed and she groaned inwardly, realising she'd phrased that badly. But he nodded and seemed not to link her remark with the fact that she'd married a wealthy man. 'At least you know where your talents lie,' he said solemnly. 'That's the main thing. Mine is management. I'm secretly hoping that if I stay away from Brazil a few days longer my directors will discover how much they need me!' He grinned crookedly and she was surprised that he could laugh at himself.

'That's fine, then,' she said with relief. 'Stay a day or so. Be my guest.'

He touched her hand and looked deeply into her eyes. 'Thank you, Ellen,' he said simply. 'I'm grateful for this time to adjust to the fact that my family is losing the estate. When you sell, I'll be quite content, I assure you.' He waited for her to comment but she kept quiet and he stretched lazily. 'This must be the first time I've taken a holiday in years. I'm a bit of a workaholic,' he admitted. 'Yes, a little holiday. Perhaps a week or so.' Looking around with a self-satisfied expression, he wasn't aware that she had tensed with irritation. 'Quiet, isn't it?' he mused. 'Like the grave.'

'Unfortunate choice of words,' she muttered. 'I don't want to be reminded of graves.'

'Of course not. Sorry.' He patted her hand sympathetically and kept a firm grip on it. 'What shall we do first? We could hit the shops in Funchal tomorrow and take tea at Reid's ——'

'I'd planned to take me and my hire car off into the mountains,' she said hastily.

'And you afraid of heights? Good grief, Ellen, you must let me drive you this first trip. The roads need some getting used to.'

'I thought I'd drive a short way and then have a walk,' she said quickly, forestalling him.

'A *levada* walk! Wonderful idea! Don't you worry,' he said, seeing her starting to speak. 'It's all virtually on the level. You wouldn't find it strenuous. A nice little walk in the countryside. Wouldn't that be wonderful?'

Her lashes dropped to conceal her amusement. He thought she was a city girl, of course, and mischief prevented her from disillusioning him. Although she'd been determined to drive on the reportedly spectacular mountain roads, she *had* been a little scared. Going with Addan would give her an idea of what they were like before she tackled them herself.

'A stroll. Sounds nice,' she beamed.

'Nothing too rigorous,' he said in a far-away voice. 'Softly running water, mossy paths, hills clothed in mimosa.' It sounded like pure heaven. Gentle, relaxing. Just what she needed. He clasped her hand to his chest in an infuriatingly appealing way. 'We'll have a good day out: get to know one another better.'

'In a purely platonic way, of course,' she said guardedly.

'Believe me, Ellen, I don't want this new understanding to founder again,' he said with total sincerity. 'I'm aware that it almost came to a grinding halt just now, when I got carried away and kissed you.'

'So long as you don't get carried away again,' she warned. 'Or you might find yourself eyeball to eyeball with one of those carp in that pool over there.'

He grinned. 'I prefer to meet my fish when they've been lightly grilled. It's a date, then? Our walk?'

'Anything for a quiet life,' she smiled wryly, wondering if she was being stupid. But the thought of wandering in the hills with someone who knew the area was too tempting an opportunity to pass up. 'Tomorrow is another day.'

# CHAPTER FIVE

ELLEN went to bed with the glorious sound of a local tenor ringing in her ears. With deep pleasure she listened to him singing his heart out as he wended his way home, no doubt from a local bar. The aria was vaguely familiar, full of passion, richly lyrical notes and soaring crescendoes that matched her extraordinary elation.

Smiling happily, she lay very still, listening, her curtain open to the starry velvet night. When the man had gone, his voice fading into the distance, there came a peaceful silence.

Apart from the crunch of footsteps in the garden outside. She stiffened, alert, then tiptoed to the window.

Beneath two enormous magnolia trees, with the moonlight casting a silver sheen on the glossy, paddle-shaped leaves, Addan was pacing up and down, his head bowed in thought. She watched curiously, wondering what was making his face so sad. The thought of leaving the Quinta forever? she mused. If so, it was surprising that he'd accepted the inevitable with such stoicism.

He stood with his back to her and lifted his dark head slowly, looking towards the black bulk of the mountains, far beyond the valley. Something told her that she was intruding. Addan had been born here, and his ancestors. He was saying goodbye and he needed privacy at this time.

For a while, she lay in bed, her exuberance blunted as she agonised over the rights and wrongs of owning a house which had such meaning for him. Her delight in the prospect of living in the Quinta seemed to have been soured. Maybe, she thought hopefully, if they both buried the hatchet and got on *very* well in the next few days, they could come to some arrangement.

Her clenched fists uncurled and she turned over, feeling more content. Addan could buy the Quinta from her and she could find somewhere else to live. Though. . .her mouth curved into a wistful smile. . .it would have been nice to live on Madeira itself.

'Ellen! Ellen, wake up!'

'Mmm.'

Blissful silence again. No need to leap out of bed and be sweet to debtors, or persuade financiers to make her a decent offer for Bruno's collapsed businesses. Nothing but sleep, for as long as. . .

'*Ohh!*' She shot up in bed, her neck dripping with icy cold water. Her frantic eyes saw Addan, standing apologetically by the bed, a flannel in one hand and a carafe of water in the other. 'What the —— ?'

'I tried everything else I could think of,' he said innocently. 'Short of — well, more intimate arousal. Like slapping your rear,' he said hastily, seeing her eyes narrow ominously. 'It was sort of humped up, very tempting, you've no idea how I itched to —— '

'Addan!' she said, hot and bothered. 'Go away. I'm sleeping. This is my bedroom.' She noticed he was wrapped in his favourite leisure attire again — the green sheet. 'Oh, go back to your master bedroom and sleep!' she groaned, turning over and pulling the blankets up firmly.

'It's nearly eleven,' he murmured in her ear.

She rolled over in surprise and found his face hovering very close over hers. 'Oh!' she said weakly, seeing his mouth curve indolently. 'That. . .that late?'

He dropped a kiss on her sleep-soft lips. 'That late,' he said gently. 'I've been working for the last three hours.'

Her eyes dropped to the sheet. 'In that?' she asked in disbelief.

'I got hot and had a shower,' he said casually. 'And

before you ask, I'd been sorting plants out in the
greenhouse. I was about to get dressed into something
tidier when I thought I'd better give you a wake-up call
so you could get yourself ready. We're missing out on a
glorious day. But if you want to stay in bed. . .' he
began, his voice growing huskier by the second.

'No!' She dropped her eyes and stared at her fingers,
which seemed to be gripping the sheets as if she'd fall
off the earth if she let go. 'No,' she repeated less wildly.
'I'm keen to explore.' His intake of breath made her
elaborate quickly. 'The hills,' she said, and felt the
tension in him. '*Levadas*,' she burbled. 'A nice, brisk
walk would do us both good, I'm sure.'

She groaned. God, she sounded like a pre-war
nanny!

Addan plainly thought so too, because his eyes were
laughing at her. 'Are you getting up at once, or am I
hauling you out of bed?' he threatened mildly.

His shoulders gleamed in the morning sunshine and
her fingers clutched the sheets even more tightly to stop
them from caressing the smooth skin. It won't do! she
told herself. He's as dangerous as ever.

'I'm getting up,' she said with amazing control. She
even managed a cheery smile. 'So go away, do, and let
a girl get her face on for the day.'

'Don't bother,' he murmured, kissing her mouth
again. 'You look fabulous as you are. Fabulous. . .'
The kiss became another. And another. And went on
forever.

Ellen's frantic fingers gave up their protesting flutters
and drifted to his shoulders, revelling in the rich feel of
his body and the clean, newly showered smell of him.
Sinking beneath his weight as he deepened the kiss in
earnest, she wondered dreamily if this was the same
woman who'd walked in on Addan the day before.

Her whole body tensed. Addan felt her sudden anger
and lifted himself up, lazily viewing her with drugged
eyes. 'What's wrong, sweetheart?' he husked lovingly.

But she knew he was playing false, of course.

'"Sweetheart"! What about your blonde?' she said jerkily.

'Maybe I've come to my senses,' he answered, his face deadly earnest.

Her wary eyes questioned him. 'Don't tell lies. You love her,' she reminded him harshly.

'I don't think I do.'

'Isn't that rather sudden?' she suggested, ice in her voice at his fickle nature.

'Not really. Sometimes, a word, a thought or a deed can trigger a reaction that changes behaviour,' he said quietly. 'You've done that. You've made me think out my future very carefully.'

The image of Addan walking, thinking and brooding during the previous night came to Ellen's mind. 'I'm glad you've decided to turn away from someone you can't marry. But that doesn't mean you're free to play the field with any woman of your choice,' she said with asperity.

'I know,' he said helplessly. 'You were just so tempting.' His finger traced the edges of her mouth and she quivered. Addan groaned. 'Quite irresistible,' he sighed. 'All that pale gold skin, unblemished, glowing,' he marvelled, his hand smoothing over her bare shoulders. 'You looked drowsy and nuzzleable. *Al dente*.'

His teeth lightly and briefly closed over the soft warm flesh below her collarbone and Ellen had to steel her body against the stabs of excitement that rocketed through her body.

'Please! I'm not breakfast! *Al dente*,' she said, managing a small woman-of-the-world laugh. 'Chewable? Like spaghetti?'

'Let me see.' His teeth began a determined assault of every inch of exposed skin and Ellen's body arched before she could stop it. Addan pulled back hastily, his dark eyes soft with hot ardour. 'Oh, God, Ellen!' he breathed. 'This is worrying. I could get very serious about you.'

There was a long silence. Her heart beat so loud that its resonances seemed to fill her whole breast. And, perhaps as if knowing this, Addan unwound the hand that gripped his shoulder and laid it on his chest. Her eyes shot wide open.

'Addan!' she gasped, astonished at the rapid, heavy pounding beneath her palm.

He nodded ruefully. 'Steam-hammer,' he admitted. 'Shortage of hearts available so I had this fitted last night instead. Will it do?'

Her lips curved into an irrepressible smile, which faded rapidly into anxiety. 'Temporary measures are never satisfactory,' she said huskily.

'Steam-hammers are built to last,' he said and pressed her palm against his lips. He rose from the bed, staring down on her with smouldering eyes. 'To be honest,' he said, 'I feel as if I've been hit by a steam-hammer myself. I don't know what's happening to me — to us,' he said, with an intimacy that made every inch of her quiver, 'but I think I'd better leave before my feelings get out of hand.' He gave her a shaky grin.

'Don't jump to any conclusions about this,' she told him as evenly as she could. 'It's a lovely morning, we're making a few changes in our attitudes towards one another and we're both feeling a bit disorientated.'

'Sure,' he said, sounding a little relieved. 'Man, woman, alone in Eden, what can you expect?'

'Snakes,' she said ruefully.

Addan grinned. 'You're quite right not to trust me,' he said approvingly. 'Men can be the very devil, can't they?' He walked to the door and she wondered if he was as innocent as he sounded. 'Don't be long. Get some breakfast into you and come into the garden ——'

'To meet the snake?' she teased.

'Ouch!' he winced, looking hurt. 'Try a little harder to see me as your would-be friend, Ellen,' he sighed.

'I want to,' she said honestly. 'I'm a bit unsure ——'

'I can understand that.' He fixed her with his fathomless black eyes. 'Perhaps I can persuade you to think about me in a different way today.'

'Depends what form your persuasion takes,' she replied quietly.

'Well, I'm terrified of those goldfish, so. . .no sudden moves, then!' he said with a laugh. It deepened into a warm chuckle. 'If you could see how wary you look. . .!'

'Don't spoil it for me,' she said soberly. 'It's my first proper trip out and I want to enjoy it.' And she didn't have the mental strength to face any more adversity.

'I hope you will,' he said convincingly. 'I'll try to make it unforgettable.'

'Uneventful will do,' she said wryly.

Addan's eyes twinkled. 'That's for butterflies. We want a bit of excitement in our lives, don't we?'

'I'll settle for dullness today,' she said firmly.

'Coward. When you're ready to leave, give a toot on the horn of my car. You won't see it from the drive, but it's parked by the dragon tree behind the magnolias.'

'OK,' she smiled, her eyes sparkling with antici-pation. He walked briskly out and she was left to blow hot and cold about her feelings for Addan till she decided she'd give him the benefit of the doubt.

It was only when she pressed the horn on the big Range Rover that she began to get cold feet about spending the next few hours in Addan's company.

She needed to think through her feelings and he wasn't giving her time to do so. There was no doubt that he was highly sexed and that if she ever let him go past 'Go' she'd end up in a prison of her own making. It was important that she keep on friendly terms — but that he didn't actually *like* her too much. And she knew how to achieve that.

Dangerous, she told herself repeatedly, her hands growing clammy. This man is dangerous.

'Good grief!' he exclaimed in astonishment when he saw her. 'Where did you get those clothes from?'

'These old things?' Affecting an offhand tone, she

surveyed her honey-coloured tracksuit and trainers. They were the most gorgeous she could find, a colour that made her complexion sing and turned her eyes a deep violet. Why had she chosen the outfit? she'd wondered as she'd slipped into it with satisfaction and bafflement.

'Those old things,' he drawled in mock-agreement.

'Amazing I kept them, really. We tried the nature kick a few years back,' she said casually. 'You know how one does.'

'I know,' he said, politely smoothing away the sardonic curl to his upper lip. 'Pretty headband. Nice colours.'

Ellen smiled to herself at his attempt to flatter what he imagined to be a vain woman. He was trying hard, but couldn't disguise his natural contempt for the kind of person he imagined her to be. She didn't blame him. She loathed women whose sole topic of conversation was clothes.

Her hand touched the twisted-rope scarves she'd wound in her hair in what she hoped was a smug gesture. 'Gold's my favourite colour,' she told him ingenuously.

'It suits you,' he agreed drily.

She smiled vacuously at him, her eyes darkening a little at the striking picture he made, standing against the backdrop of the rich green hills. He wore black cords and a body-hugging cotton-knit shirt in taupe, a similar-coloured cashmere sweater elegantly knotted around his shoulders. Very co-ordinated. Classically Continental, sexy. She decided not to tell him so. Her voice would be too revealing.

'I'm so glad you think so. Now, tell me where we're going,' she said crisply, finding her fluttering girly role boring already.

Diving into the back-pocket of his cords, he brought out a map and opened it out on the bonnet of the car. 'Here, back along the new road towards Funchal and across the Socorridos. . .' His finger traced a deep ravine '. . .then up the gorge — lovely drive, very typical — to Eira do Serrado — I'll leave its description as a surprise — and on to Curral das Freiras, a village deep in the mountains.'

Ellen could hardly hold back her excitement. 'Looks wonderful!' she exclaimed. 'But the road finishes there. Where do we go from there?'

'We'll have to come back the same way. No vehicles can get through the mountains beyond. Worth it, though. You'll see. We'll do a *levada* walk at Curral. I know a good one.' He began to fold up the map and then paused, looking at her quizzically. 'You'll have to map-read. There's been some road-building since I was here last and I'm a bit hazy on the route around the first section.'

Her face fell. She'd followed his stabbing finger, but actually reading the names would be a strain and he'd laugh at her attempts to decipher the words. 'Oh, dear! I'm not very good —— ' she began doubtfully.

'Oh, the reading. Your little problem. No, of course not!' he smiled, patting her cheek. 'I was forgetting. Bruno said you could only manage pictures.'

'Bruno did?' she asked, aghast. It had been her secret.

'Oh, he told me a lot about you.' Addan's thoughtful eyes dwelled on her as if enjoying her anxiety. 'Don't worry. I can handle the map-reading. You just sit and admire the scenery.'

Hating to feel stupid, Ellen nodded dutifully. 'Anything you say, Addan.'

His eyes flicked over to her briefly. 'We're taking the Alfa Romeo,' he murmured. 'I thought you'd prefer it. More glamorous. We can float around the hairpin bends and drive with the hood down. It shouldn't disturb your hair too much,' he said in a kindly tone.

She flung him a smile, beginning to worry about the journey. Bruno had told her about the magnificent views. Views meant heights. Hairpin bends meant nerve-racking drops beside the road. But she'd known

that, and she'd been determined to overcome her
nervousness about heights. Living on a mountainous
island, she'd have to!

There was a sense of thrill and anticipation about the
journey as she let Addan hand her into the gleaming
silver bullet of a car he'd brought out from the garage.
So much was changing for her in her life; an upsurge of
hope surrounded her and she began to hum happily to
the pop-opera tunes on the car's stereo system.

Addan drove beautifully, the car was a dream, and
she adored the sensation of having the wind blowing
through her hair.

'Not too much, with the hood down, is it?' he called
to her, his face glowing with a heart-stopping elation.

'No! I love it! Wonderful fresh air, tang of the sea,
scent of that white stuff,' she cried, pointing to the star-
shaped flowers drifting on the wind from billowing trees
beside the road and showering them in blossom.

'Pittosporum,' he told her. 'You look like a bride,' he
added huskily. He smoothed down her hair, and the
scented flowers fell to her shoulders.

Surrounded in a wonderful perfume, Ellen lifted her
ecstatic face to the morning sun and her hair streamed
back, making her feel intensely alive, as if she were
setting out on a big adventure. 'I must get a plant and
flower book,' she said eagerly, keen to try to identify
some of the incredible plants by the wayside.

'I would have thought that was hardly worthwhile, if
you're going after a week or so,' he suggested, a slight
frown creasing his bronze forehead.

She nodded in hasty agreement and reminded herself
not to make thoughtless remarks till she felt sufficiently
sure of him to discuss the matter of the house.

The road descended from the vine-clad foothills to
the banana belt, skirting dramatic ravines and offering
breathtaking views of the snow-capped mountains on
one side and the sea on the other. Then it began to
climb up again, winding up steeply in a rapid series of
stomach-swooping hairpin bends.

'Ohh!' she gasped, gripping the edge of her seat, as Addan deftly threaded his car between the sheer rock-face and an oncoming lorry carrying giant boulders.

'Nervous?' he murmured, glancing at her.

'Watch the road! Watch the road!' she cried sharply.

'Terraces on your left,' he said, waving a casual hand as they came to another blind bend. 'Potatoes, I think. Four crops a year from this soil, you know.'

'Both hands on the wheel, if you don't mind,' she said, her breath shallow with apprehension.

'OK. And,' he added, with the car now close to the edge of a sheer five-hundred-foot drop, 'down there. . . can you see the sugar cane?'

'Watch the corner!' she husked in a strained voice.

'I am,' he said amiably. 'My family got rich from sugar cane. We had sugar mills in the fifteenth century when sugar commanded high prices in Europe.'

'Really?' she squeaked, as he swerved to avoid a small pothole and the car pointed itself towards the abyss.

'Mmm.' His strong hands corrected the steering effortlessly. 'A lot of our paintings came from Bruges, as swaps for sugar. And the sugar-crate furniture, made from the beautiful wood —'

'Fascinating,' she said weakly, wishing he'd stop talking and attend to his driving. Her stomach was leaping up and down like a yo-yo.

'Knew you'd be interested.' His hand rested briefly on her knee and she tried to tense it, but her legs were too busy doing an impression of soft-set jelly. 'You're trembling!' he said in consternation.

'Am I?' she said in a high, trembly little voice.

Addan slowed down and parked the car at a purpose-built viewing-point beside a riot of poinsettias.

'What a wonderful view!' croaked Ellen, wishing she could appreciate it better. But her stomach was now somewhere around her feet. She looked further ahead into the distance, at the steeply sloping terraces, and felt a little better. Then Addan's hand was cupping the side of her cheek and turning her head around to face him.

'You're scared,' he said, turning off the engine.

Ellen breathed a sigh of relief that they were stationary at last and let some of her tension go. 'A bit,' she admitted. He took hold of her aching, curled fingers, opened them out gently and massaged them, a thoughtful look on his face. It was stupid, pretending. Any fool could tell she was nervous. 'It's nothing,' she said, giving a little laugh. 'Only white-knuckle scared.'

He hesitated, studying her pale face and brave 'I'm OK really' smile. 'You should have said heights bothered you *that* much,' he chided. 'I thought you were kidding.'

'I wish I were,' she husked.

'Ellen! I would have chosen somewhere less dramatic than this route. You know,' he said gently, 'it's a good thing you're not intending to live here! Imagine driving around these roads yourself!'

Her unhappy eyes blinked up at him. 'Imagine!' she whispered in dismay.

There was a noticeable tensing of his body and his eyes became a lake of secrets. 'Oh, dear. You're not thinking of living in the Quinta, are you?' he asked gently. 'The way you are about these roads, you'd never be able to go anywhere —'

'I would!' she frowned, privately worried about the implications. 'I'd get used to them in time,' she said stubbornly.

'To hell with the roads; you'd hate the whole environment,' he retorted. 'This isn't Filofax country, you know, and the social life is very different from what you're used to. We have fun here, but not with such. . . such a frantic wildness.'

Crossly she jerked her head away, only to be faced with a drop into oblivion, just yards away. Her stomach turned to water and she glowered down at her hands, twisting around his. 'I wouldn't hate it!' she denied, lifting her gaze back to the breathtakingly beautiful ravine. 'Besides, isn't it my business where I live?'

'But if you can't drive along —— '

'I will!' she said grimly.

'So you mean to settle here.'

'I might.'

He let out his breath slowly. 'That would be very foolish,' he said quietly. 'Why do you persist in doing things that aren't right for you? You belong on some wealthy man's arm, decorating his house and enlivening his bed. Perhaps somewhere like Monaco, or Nice. Not Madeira.'

'You don't know what's best for me,' she said vehemently. 'If I want to stay here I will and I won't let vertigo beat me. I don't let *anything* beat me. I'll show you.'

Snatching her hands from his, she opened the car door and forced herself outside, edging along the side of the silver-grey Alfa Romeo till she was close to the rustic fence that separated her from a verdant valley, far below.

The pain in her loins was sharp, but she was sure her nervousness could be conquered. It had to be. Using every scrap of her courage and concentration, she stared hard at the rich cinnamon-coloured soil below and listened to the sound of trickling water running beside the road and the warm hum of bees on their frenzied forays into the mimosa trees. The fluffy pom-pom flowers were creating carpets of yellow all over the verges. It was really pretty, she told herself fiercely.

The car door slammed and Addan joined her, his arm strong and supportive around her shoulder. 'My tough little cookie,' he murmured. 'Aversion therapy,' he murmured. 'What a good idea.'

'Pardon?'

He smiled at her. 'Did I get that wrong?' he asked innocently. 'I mean, if you become familiar with a fear, you master it. Let's give it a try and you'll find out if you can cope with everyday life in Madeira.'

'I'll do it on my own——'

'Better with me. I've got hold of you, there's a rail stopping you from hurtling down into the valley, so you're quite safe. Isn't it a long way?' he marvelled, craning his neck forward and edging her closer. 'What's that down there?'

Without thinking, she looked—and wished she hadn't, burying her face in his shoulder and then irritably pulling back again, to stare wide-eyed and petrified into the mid-distance.

'A man working,' she said tremulously.

Addan leant forward to check. 'So it is. Must be a thousand feet below and he's on a forty-five-degree slope. Amazing. And what good eyesight you've got!'

His movement had made her lose her balance a little. The rush of fear swooped to claim her insides as he came upright again. 'Ohh! Keep *still*!' she said through her teeth.

'Sorry. We'll stand here for a few moments and you can enjoy the view and let your stomach settle down.' He gave her a sympathetic grin. 'I expect it's turning over and over, isn't it?'

Ellen was preoccupied with her wobbly legs. 'Don't you get a swooping feeling when you look down?' she asked resentfully.

'No. But Madeirans are born with an inbred lack of fear of heights. Survival of the fittest, I suppose. Those who fell, jumped or went mad just died out and we're left with the fearless and the agile,' he joked.

She took a deep, steadying breath. 'Help me,' she said tensely. Her face lifted to his in a silent plea. 'This is a lovely place and I want to enjoy it. I need to conquer my fear, Addan.'

His jaw tightened and the arms around her did too. 'I'll do my best,' he promised huskily. 'I do admire you,' he said in a caressing tone. 'You stand on the edge of danger and face it head-on.' He kissed her forehead. 'There's a little more to you than meets the eye, isn't there?' he said thoughtfully.

'Only my thermal vest,' she joked, desperate to convince him that she was as deep as a puddle.

He laughed and helped her back into the car again. But he remained thoughtful and she sensed peril for herself.

'Funny thing about danger,' he mused, driving off, 'it can put fear in your heart, but there's a kind of excitement about it, too.' He glanced across at her, his eyes speculative. 'Ever watch a horror movie and been so scared that you couldn't bear to look — but felt utterly compelled to stay with it to the bitter end?'

'Heavens,' she demurred shakily, 'that's too deep for me!'

He smiled faintly and made no comment. But she knew what he was getting at. Addan was danger itself, yet he excited her. And she felt compelled to know what his intentions were. Was that it? she wondered. The reason why she was so attracted to him?

The thrill of excitement, the risk of the unknown, like stepping off a cliff. That was the rushing, headlong sensation she got with the unpredictable, secretive Addan. Intuitively she knew he'd never fully shown his innermost self to anyone and it was his ability to stand alone that drew her like a magnet. He seemed so insular, so utterly complete in himself that it was almost inhuman.

And the effect on her was remarkable. He had a gift of making her afraid, to cause her stomach to clench with nerves. And when she looked at him sometimes, he had the knack of suggesting that she'd drop into a deep, bottomless chasm if she fell into his arms and risked letting herself go.

Danger, fear, excitement. Yes, that summed up Addan perfectly. And she longed to reach out to him, towards the dark excitement.

Hiding her fears — on all counts — she chatted with reasonable composure as Addan drove along the tortuous road beside tall eucalyptus groves. And their easy conversation relaxed her as he described his life in Rio.

Work, work and more work, it seemed, and she wondered why, though the stories of his trips inland to visit his mines in the Amazon were fascinating.

When they stopped again, and strolled in a companionable way along a path to the Eira do Serrado — whatever that was — she felt as if the stress of years was slipping away.

'Serrado,' said Addan proudly, propelling her forward with a hand that brooked no resistance. But Ellen's sudden indrawn breath caused him to slide that hand down to her bottom and give it a reassuring little pat. 'You want to find out if you can live here, this is the place to do it.'

He'd left her. Mercifully, she could flatten herself against a rock, the tension flowing back with a vengeance. 'Oh, my God!' she breathed, too petrified to be angry at his patronising treatment of her.

It was a viewpoint; a platform protected by a rustic rail and built out from the rock-face over. . . She closed her eyes. Nothing.

'It's OK. Look, quite safe,' called Addan cheerfully.

She opened one eye and blanched. He stood right on the edge, unafraid, smiling. 'I'll stay here, thanks.'

'Afraid that rock's going to run away?' he goaded. 'Claiming it for the English nation, or something?'

Anger straightened her. 'OK, clever. So you have nerves of steel. Mine have rusted.'

'We're over three thousand feet up, you know,' he said in a conversational tone. 'It would be quite something if you were brave enough to look down to the valley below.'

'It would be a miracle. Miracles take a while to organise. Let me do this in my own time,' she muttered, taking one cautious step forward. Her fingertips remained in contact with the rock. Just in case something moved. Addan, the ground, the mountain. . . Oh, heavens, she thought angrily, she *was* stupid!

'Well done,' Addan said gently. 'You're doing fine. Keep touching base. . .and look. It's a stupendous sight, Ellen, one you must see.' He chuckled. 'Far more interesting than your feet, dainty and perfectly formed though they may be.'

Slowly her eyes lifted from the ground, her legs braced as if the platform was swaying — which it was, as far as her head was concerned.

'Oh!' she sighed in awe, and ventured further to see more, her arms outstretched like a sleepwalker. Her eyes slanted to Addan, daring him to laugh but he seemed rather subdued.

'Compelling, isn't it?' He leaned nonchalantly on the rail, watching her.

'Irresistible,' she agreed. 'But I'm still scared.'

He grinned broadly as if she'd said something funny. 'One more step. There are some beautiful red aloes, growing on the edge here,' came his low, coaxing voice. 'And you've just got to see the cliff-hanging terraces this side.'

'Terraces? On these slopes? Good grief, what do these people do in their leisure time — climb Everest?' Addan's grin didn't help her knees much. He looked really devastatingly handsome when he smiled, she mused. And he'd been doing that a lot lately.

'Here, if there isn't any land, we make it with our bare hands. Madeirans are a stubborn people ——'

'You can say that again,' she muttered.

'Any area less than vertical gets pressed into service.' He looked bland enough but there was an undeniable pride in his voice. 'Have a look,' he encouraged. 'These terraces were built by muscle and brawn. Soil was brought up a thousand feet or more on the backs of men, load by load. And the villagers climb up to sow and till the ground regularly and then climb down again with the crop, bag by bag. It's astounding. Come and see.'

Intrigued and repelled at the same time, she bit her lip. 'I must,' she said to herself.

'Take a deep breath and let it go.' His voice took on the consistency of liquid velvet. 'Move forward on the outward breath. Your stomach won't have room to cramp if your lungs are empty.'

Her huge blue eyes met his. Drawn by their quiet command, she did as he said. For a few seconds she forgot her fear. The view below took her breath away, anyway.

She looked down on the upper terraces, which seemed totally inaccessible, and marvelled at the tough will of the men who'd built and worked them. 'That's what I call determination,' she said, her voice low with awe.

'That's what *I* call determination,' he agreed softly.

He meant her, she realised with pleasure! And, to her dismay, she blushed as if his approval was important. 'It's not the sole prerogative of Madeirans,' she said wryly, turning back to the scene before her.

'So I see,' came his warm response.

And she glowed. Instinctively, Addan seemed to know she had to have space around her and wisely left her alone, staying very still while gradually, cautiously, she edged around the platform — still a few feet from the edge — in little shuffling steps, smiles wreathing her face.

'It's quite, quite magical,' she husked dreamily, wishing she had the nerve to peer right down, to the very bottom.

'If magic can be caused by pure force,' he murmured.

Puzzled by his tone, she glanced at him, her face still filled with wonder, and this time it was his expression of tenderness that caused her heart to somersault. 'An earthquake, you mean?' she said, feeling suddenly shaky. It was as if the ground shook beneath her own feet. Addan had never looked at her with such affectionate warmth before. Heat began to flow through her body and she tried to behave normally. 'Or a volcanic eruption?' she croaked.

'No.' His mouth curved into a generous smile that weakened her knees. 'Water,' he said softly, his mouth infinitely seductive to her startled eyes. 'Are you paying attention, Ellen?'

'Mmm.' Incapable of coherent speech, she nodded perkily. 'Go on.'

He gave her a long, slow look and she felt giddy. 'The water came from the snow-melt in the far-distant past,' he continued huskily. 'It had one aim and one only and it flowed over any obstacle in its way ——'

'You do that,' she said shakily.

'Perhaps we both do.' A silence, long and tense, followed his quietly drawled words. Ellen placed her hand on her chest in a gesture that said, What, little me? and Addan laughed in delight — and disbelief. 'OK. But I think we're alike in believing that seduction gets you more places than outright hostility.'

Worrying about his meaning, she shrugged her shoulders. 'You were telling me about the river,' she said with sugary sweetness.

'I was, wasn't I?' he said suavely. 'In Zarco's day, the rush of water was so tremendous where it surged into the sea that it almost wrecked his ship.'

'I've got to see this amazing river!' She expected a downstream Niagara at least. Her hand touched the rail — she'd got that close! she thought in amazement. She took a huge breath and slowly let it out. Peering over, right to the bottom of the gorge, she saw the river far below, a silver thread glinting in the sun. 'Oh. It looks tame,' she said, her disappointed eyes lifting to Addan's.

'Merely an illusion,' he murmured, his mouth quirking. 'When you get near enough, you'll see how turbulent it is. Quite dangerous.' His hand rested lightly on her shoulder. 'Look more closely. See those boulders?'

'I can't,' she said reluctantly.

'I'll hold you around the waist.'

His arm was there before she could protest and so she obediently leaned out to get the moment over with. She compared the boulders with the size of the buildings and blinked.

'Huge! They must have been tossed around like ping-pong balls!' she exclaimed, returning to the vertical and peeling off his fingers, one by one.

'We'll go down there in a moment and I'll show you.'

'By jumping?' she suggested with a theatrical roll of her eyes.

He laughed. 'You'd be jam if you jumped!' Ellen shuddered and his hand caressed her shoulder to calm her. 'Trust me. We'll get there safely, I promise you,' he said reassuringly. 'But while we're here you must see the whole panorama. People have expended a lot of energy making this platform. You might as well make full use of it. Take your time.' His eyes shimmered with amusement. 'Go back and grab the rock again, if you think that'll keep it in place.'

He made her giggle at his teasing and she promised herself that she'd see everything. It would be too shaming if she turned tail now, with Addan mocking her lack of nerve.

'You challenge me, Addan Machico de Torre,' she said with a defiant tilt to her head, 'and my stubborn streak will rise to the occasion!'

'I thought it might,' he replied smugly.

Her pretend glare made him laugh and for a few brief seconds they smiled at one another in almost a form of friendship. Then Ellen dragged her attention back to the magnificence of the almost completely encircling rugged mountains, the beautiful 'lost world' ravine — and, incredibly, a sizeable village of little white houses.

'You're doing remarkably well,' said Addan, draping his arm around her shoulders and giving her a quick, friendly hug.

She nodded with pleasure but kept a tight hold on the rail and her stomach. 'I can't believe I'm up here,' she admitted. 'And not a gibbering wreck. But it *is* unmissable! And what a setting for a village! There doesn't seem to be a road to it at all!'

'Lean over and this time do it all on your own without my support. You'll see the road disappearing into a tunnel.'

'Not again. My insides ache.'

Addan turned her chin to him and kissed her parted lips tenderly. 'Coward.'

'I know what you're doing,' she frowned. 'You're daring me again.'

He kissed her once more. 'Now in these circumstances,' he said calmly, 'I am more at ease and can therefore move faster than you. I intend to kiss you,' he said, deepening the next kiss, 'until you lean over and look. If you should try to move away, I'll cut off your retreat. Nasty, aren't I?' His laughing face hovered close to hers.

'You said it,' she muttered. Her pout was covered expertly by Addan's questing lips. Wonderful, she thought. 'This is awful!' she said sharply. 'You're blackmailing me! You know I don't like being kissed——'

'Then you'll obviously choose to do as I ask, won't you?' he said smugly.

'You get your own way whatever I choose,' she protested.

'Yes,' he said, infuriatingly self-satisfied. 'I always like to give people a choice of things I want them to do.' His eyes gleamed and she sensed that this was a policy he carried out in the whole of his life. Kisses or stomach-churning terror. What a choice—especially when she knew which she *really* preferred.

'Rat,' she said darkly, pushing at his steadying arms. 'Of course I'll do it. Don't rush me. I need to pluck up the courage again.'

Several deep breaths and a couple of false starts later, she managed to get as far as placing her hands on the rails, bracing her body against them and testing their strength while the enviably confident Addan leaned casually against them, arms folded, an amused expression on his face.

Ellen ignored him. And leaned out a little way. . . then more. Fear and excitement shot through her bloodstream, making her feel light-headed. Whoopee! she went inside. She was doing this all on her own!

'I can see the road — and the tunnel!' she cried, her eyes sparkling, jamming back the urge to let out the whoopee and hear it echo around the mountains. 'There's more of the village further down, at the bottom of the ravine!'

'The village is the Curral das Freiras.'

She dared not turn her head. Any movement would unnerve her totally. So she yelled into the pure mountain air. 'The nuns'. . .?'

'Shelter,' he provided, watching in approval as she eagerly scanned the houses, lying in the shadows of the great mountains behind them. 'The nuns came from the Santa Clara Convent during the sixteenth century when pirates raided Funchal. They fled to the hills and stumbled on this secret valley.'

'Some nuns!' she laughed.

'We have a long history of muscled thighs,' chuckled Addan. One of his shifted close against her leg and she stiffened but didn't dare move. 'There wasn't a road to it till recently. For centuries,' he continued, unaware of the effect his burning body was having on her, 'people were born, lived and died here, without ever leaving the valley.'

Ellen's hands gripped the rail, her knuckles bone-white. 'What an astonishing thought!' Her huge eyes lifted to the massive sunlit mountains which curved around the village like a wall. 'Are the mountains keeping the villagers in, or the world out?' she wondered aloud. 'Your whole world, bounded by rock,' she mused. 'Wars, plagues, earth-shattering events, all passing you by. The coming of the road must have made quite a difference.'

Addan murmured in agreement, his hand stroking her arm absently. 'Hard to imagine what it must have been like for them. I bet some refused to go out into the wide world. And there must have been a lot of heart-searching about letting strangers into their sanctuary, too — and the possible corrupting influences.'

She was silent, thinking of how she had run for sanctuary by coming to Madeira. But somehow she'd stumbled on perhaps greater dangers and worries than she'd faced before in the shape of her fatally attractive, fatally flawed brother-in-law.

# CHAPTER SIX

ADDAN'S arms tightened around her and suddenly Ellen had the sensation that despite everything there were moments with him, like now, leaning against his strong, secure body, when she felt protected and encircled. He'd even shown some insight into the villagers' plight when faced with the double-edged sword of progress.

The serenity of their surroundings stole over them both. They stood together, enthralled by the dramatic beauty of the scenery, for some time not breaking the hush that surrounded them. Ellen inhaled the crisp, clean air and felt wonderfully exhilarated by her progress in coping with her vertigo, and the unexpected sense of space and freedom.

'I love this place,' she said huskily, looking around at him. Her face was a little too close to his and she turned back as quickly as she could without revealing how he affected her. 'The more I stay here,' she mused, 'the less afraid I am. Thanks for bullying me.'

'My pleasure!' His eyes gleamed beneath the hooded lids.

'I'm sure,' she said drily.

'Of course,' he murmured, 'I was only doing it to see how far you'd go.'

'As far as I have to for my own satisfaction,' she said amused by his admission. 'Well, whatever your reason, it worked. And no one's ever been this patient with me before. I am grateful, despite your dubious motives.'

'How are your pulses?' he enquired softly, turning her hand over on the rail. Deprived of one anchor, she cringed against him and his arm tightened around her waist. 'It's OK, I've got you,' he said, believing that was reassuring. Beneath his testing finger, she felt the rapid, heavy pounding of her treacherously excitable blood. 'Oh, dear! I detect terror,' he drawled.

The wonderful strength of his body was tempting her beyond endurance. She wanted to turn from the view and cling on to him, but she was so confused by her emotions that she knew she couldn't trust herself just to cling. There'd be a few sighs of relief, an abandoning of her stiff upper lip, and he'd take advantage of that.

'Terror?' she repeated, sounding strained, his gently caressing fingers sending shivers along her skin. 'That's not terror, it's hysteria!' she said, seeking refuge in humour. 'I'm scared half to death.'

'Oh, Ellen!' he murmured, gently turning her around. 'How well you hide your inner fears.' I've had to, she thought sadly, wishing there had been someone to take them away. 'You're remarkable. I'm glad we came. Perhaps you'll trust me a little more willingly. That was my main aim. Nothing bad happened, did it?'

'I suppose I should be grateful you didn't heave me over the edge!' she said ruefully.

He clapped a hand to his forehead. 'I *knew* I'd forgotten to do something!' His eyes glinted wickedly at her. 'Never mind,' he murmured, waggling a melodramatic eyebrow. 'There'll be plenty of other opportunities!'

'How can I be sure of trusting you,' she complained, 'when you keep making remarks like that?'

'You can't. After all,' he said with a mock-evil leer, 'if you should have a fatal accident, I'll inherit your fortune.'

Ellen burst into peals of laughter at the thought of a murderous Addan discovering she had no fortune, and he looked at her curiously. 'Don't ask,' she giggled, at his querying eyebrow. 'Don't ask!'

'A mystery. I love mysteries,' he murmured. 'I thrive on intrigue and excitement. Speaking of which, you look as if someone's pumped a magnum of champagne directly into your veins.'

Her sparkling eyes met his. 'I feel elated, that's why,'

she smiled happily. 'I've achieved a lot. I seem to have taken a step towards opening up my life. I always resented not going up mountains or enjoying drives along mountain roads. I never learnt to ski because of that and I dearly wanted to. Oddly enough, it was terribly exciting back there.'

'Exhilarating,' he agreed softly.

'Have you ever been thrilled at achieving something you've wanted badly for a long time?' she asked absently, as they walked back to the car.

'Oh, yes.'

The enigmatic, far-away smile that appeared on his mouth left her guessing. Was it a woman he'd finally seduced? she wondered, feeling a rush of sympathy for all the unknown, helpless females who'd fallen hopelessly for the smooth, suave and fickle Addan.

Yet she could still marvel at the adrenalin surging through her body. Something had stirred all her old exuberance back into life. It was as though she'd been in a dark room for years and someone had switched her on and created an electrical charge inside her.

'I have an overwhelming urge to do cartwheels,' she blurted out, almost skipping beside him.

'No one's stopping you.'

Ellen caught a shadowy expression flitting across his eyes and sobered a little. 'Mucky ground,' she said, trying to regain some of her discarded priggish image. 'Don't want to break a nail, do I?'

To her surprise, he seemed disappointed. 'Heaven forfend!' he said drily.

She smiled, but felt wary again. How much did he know about her? Had he guessed that she was trying — rather unsuccessfully — to play the parasitic socialite? Addan was so darn granite-faced sometimes, she thought irritably, that it was hard knowing what went on in that fathoms-deep mind of his.

Ellen's new courage was tested to its limit on the road to the Curral. But Addan drove carefully, with constant changing of gear, on the perilously twisting road hacked out of the side of the mountain and which disappeared into low, dark tunnels that dripped water on the car roof.

At the very bottom of the ravine, it was like being in another place entirely: silent, balmy, tranquillity itself. Her feet hit solid ground and nothing trembled any more, not even her hand, firmly held in Addan's as he courteously helped her out.

She looked up at the wall of sheer mountains towering above them, a contented smile on her face.

'Safe at last,' said Addan softly, reading her thoughts. 'Nothing to worry about here.' A faint smile touched his lips and disappeared. 'Ready for that walk now? I brought some food, thinking we might stop on the path and have a picnic.'

Ellen thought briefly of the bread and ham she'd bought on her way from the airport and hoped he'd put in some fruit. 'Smashing!' she said enthusiastically, gazing around in delight. Here she could cope. Addan was quite enough to handle, without sheer drops to confuse the issue. 'Isn't it glorious?' she sighed.

The shadow touched his eyes again. 'Glorious,' he agreed, turning to lift out a small rucksack. 'I'll put your waterproof in,' he said casually.

'There's blue sky!'

'You never know what's going to happen once you're in mountain country,' he said softly. 'You can be walking along in bright sunshine one minute and in thick mist the next. Treacherous places, mountains. Never trust them, Ellen. Always have contingency plans.'

A little alarmed, she looked up at his blandly innocent face as he hitched the rucksack on to his broad shoulders. 'I hope nothing spoils our walk,' she said in a low, warning tone. 'All I wanted was a taste of the real Madeira.'

'You'll get that,' he promised her, smiling. 'I just wanted to prepare you for all eventualities.' He offered his hand in such a friendly way that she couldn't refuse to take it. 'We go up here.'

Ellen's adrenalin was running again. Somehow she knew he wasn't really talking about rain and taking sensible clothes. He'd blown open her sense of security and put an edge to her anticipation. The walk could turn out to be uneventful — or he could have something in store for her. Either way, he'd made darn sure that her nerves were straining with the suspense!

'You ought to be making horror films,' she said drily, as they strolled beside an osier bed. 'You've got a nice line in doom and gloom.'

Addan grinned at her. 'I prefer my excitement first-hand, don't you?'

'What are you cooking up for me, Addan?' she asked warily.

'A taste of Madeira!' he said with hurt innocence. 'We're going up to the *levada* and then along the path that runs alongside it.'

'Sounds harmless.'

'You don't sound convinced!' he chuckled. 'Want to go back to the Quinta?'

'Absolutely not!' she said stoutly. 'You're not depriving me of my walk with your sinister mutterings. I can't wait to see what a *levada* looks like close up. I've only seen pictures.'

'Terrific!' he enthused, squeezing her hand and striding on so fast that she was obliged to half run to keep up. 'Not long now. How much do you know about the watercourses?'

'Only what Bruno told me.' She wrinkled her brow, trying to remember. 'He said the *levadas* were a bit like small roman aqueducts — and they were built to bring water from the mountains to the dry south of the island.'

'Did he tell you that they stretch for one thousand three hundred miles?' He grinned at her gasp of astonishment. 'Unbelievable, isn't it? Hand-built again, of course, because of the impossible terrain, sometimes by men suspended on the end of a rope dangling over a precipice, with all the sand and cement, everything necessary, carried up on men's backs.'

'Wow!' she said, deeply impressed. 'Your men are really tough.'

'We are, aren't we?' he said smugly. 'And the women,' he acknowledged. 'Mind you, the day they find a way to strap an excavator beneath a helicoptor we Madeirans will breathe a sigh of relief!'

Ellen's laughter echoed in the still warm air. 'Oh! Is that it?' she said, stopping in surprise at the low stone channel, filled with crystal-clear water. 'It's smaller than I thought.'

'This one's about a metre deep and a couple of feet wide. They vary a little — as do the widths of the paths. Some are only a foot wide where the rock was difficult to excavate. Don't forget, the paths are primarily for maintenance, not originally for walkers like us.'

She smiled happily. 'I feel like an adventurer,' she said eagerly, a little sorry that they had to walk in single file along the mossy track. The low watercourse was edged with agapanthus and lilies and someone had been planting little cuttings of hydrangeas in the bright red soil as well. She dipped her fingers in the *levada* and brought them out quickly. 'Ice cold!' she laughed, her face alight with joy.

'Move on, Ellen,' he said cheerfully. 'There's a way to go before we eat.'

For a long while they ambled beside the gurgling water, each lost in his and her own thoughts. Once the *levada* disappeared and she could hear it rushing beneath the huge flat stones under their feet. To her right, the hillside fell away comparatively gently and had been planted with vines. With their dark, twisting branches supported above head height on roughly hewn poles and a system of wires, they created a stunning pattern.

Addan picked some mimosa and tucked it into her hairband, his cool breath shimmering on her sensitive face. She looked up at him, her eyes bright as the cloudless sky.

'Oh, Ellen,' he said huskily. 'You look happier than I've ever seen you.'

'I think I am,' she answered slowly.

'Trust me?'

'Not. . .completely.'

Addan gave a rueful smile. 'I suppose I don't blame you for being cautious. But you don't hate me as you used to, do you?'

Her solemn eyes widened at the languidly sensuous expression on his face. 'No, I don't,' she said honestly.

She made to turn, alerted by the intention in his smouldering eyes, but he caught her effortlessly and spun her around. His mouth met hers in a determined embrace and she remained stiff and unreceptive while her pulses scattered in all directions.

Just as she was fighting the urge to wrap her arms around his neck and join in, he drew back, though holding her arms in a fierce grip. He seemed quite bewildered.

'OK. Mistake,' he frowned, meeting her accusing eyes. 'I could kick myself——'

'Allow me,' she said grimly, upset that he'd spoilt the pleasant, easygoing atmosphere.

He heaved a sigh. 'By all means.' He gave a short laugh. 'I'm not used to feeling. . .overjoyed,' he confessed.

Ellen blinked. Neither was she. And travelling in such a short space of time from the edge of danger and fear to the edge of danger and happiness was putting an overload on her emotions.

'Hug a tree,' she suggested shakily. 'It won't answer back.'

'I like it when you respond to me. We could have been good friends in different circumstances,' he said surprisingly.

Startled, she knew he was right. She actually liked being with him. Apart from the sexual attraction, there was something intangible that linked them. 'I'll go along with the friendship,' she said huskily. 'That's as far as I want it to go.'

'Then, friend,' he grinned, 'we have half a mile to go before we can eat lunch so let's get moving.'

The ground began to drop away a little more steeply, but there were trees on the slopes and Ellen wasn't afraid. Then, as she turned a corner, she came to a halt. Water was overflowing the *levada* channel and tumbling downhill in a foaming torrent. Earth and stone blocked their way completely.

'We can't go any further!' she called back to Addan.

He came up close to her shoulder. 'I thought the water level had dropped back there. There's been a small landslide,' he frowned. 'Nothing major. Perhaps we can go round it. . . Let me investigate.'

To her horror, he jumped with surprising agility down below the path and searched the fall of earth and boulders for a way across. Ellen glanced to beyond the landslide and saw that if they slipped on the loosened soil and rock they'd crash a few hundred feet down the hill to a clump of eucalyptus trees.

'I'm not doing that,' she said, aghast.

'I'll make you a Companion of Honour,' he coaxed, laughing up at her.

'Posthumously?' she muttered, finding the proposition unappealing.

He roared with laughter. 'Jump into my arms, you wise-cracking temptress!' he chuckled. 'You want to miss the Quatro Fontes? The great waterfalls, hurtling a thousand feet past our ears?'

'Oh. Waterfalls?'

'They're wonderful, Ellen,' he said fervently. 'Sheer ribbons of water jetting out from the cliff, down to the valley below. You can't miss them. You absolutely can't!'

'I don't want to!' she agreed. 'But. . .'

'It's not as dangerous as it looks. Once you're here, you'll see,' he wheedled.

'You do know how to coax a girl!' she said wryly, trying to judge whether she was up to the challenge or not.

'I do,' he nodded, smiling. 'And I know you're excited by the spectacular. What could be more spectacular than telling the folks back home that you crossed a landslide and walked under waterfalls?'

'Do you really think I can make it?' she asked hopefully.

'Well, I'm going across, so you'd be left to wait or go back to the car.'

'And you've got the food!' she wailed.

'I'm keeping it, too. And the car keys. Come on, Ellen. If I can, surely you can?' he said slyly.

'I do dislike men like you,' she said crossly. 'I'm supposed to be on holiday, a little light shopping, a bit of worrying about the earrings I've chosen, and where I'm going to eat tonight. Instead, I find myself suspended a few thousand feet above a valley floor, doing a Blondin tightrope act along a narrow path and now you want me to play mountain-goat games.'

'And you're loving every minute of it,' he said softly. 'Your face is glowing, your eyes are vivid, every inch of you is alive and —— '

'Alive could be a temporary state,' she said, pretending to look doubtfully at the rocks below. Her heart was already thudding with recognition that she *had* enjoyed every second. How contrary of her! She'd come for a rest! Yesterday she'd been tired, drained, mentally barren. Today she was a different person. Yet she hated heights. Why wasn't she running, screaming back up to the car?

'Alive means living,' he answered huskily, holding out his arms in a compelling invitation.

'I'm a fool,' she grumbled, sitting on the edge of the bank. 'Not only am I risking my life this once, but I'm fully aware that I've got to come back this way, too.' Before she could do anything, his hands had clamped around her waist and he was lifting her in mid-air. 'Ohh!' she screamed, terrified.

So he put her down. Slowly, all the way down the length of his hard body, his eyes seducing her inch by unbearable inch. That was worse and she almost asked him to lift her into the air again but nothing came from her mouth but a small sigh.

'We go from tree to tree,' he muttered, his gaze now locked on to her softly parted lips. His finger brushed pollen from her ear and her body melted at his drowsy dark eyes. 'We go slowly and you follow whatever I do.' His tongue touched his lips as if they were dry. Ellen knew hers were parched but didn't dare do the same.

'Sounds dodgy to me,' she croaked.

Addan gave her a look half of amusement, half exasperation. His hand exerted pressure on her spine and her nose was almost touching his chin. 'Are you running from something?' he enquired lazily.

'Not yet,' she said jerkily, alarmed at the way his husky voice was playing havoc with her nerves.

'Not scared enough?' he said throatily.

Her mutinous eyes glowered at him. 'You've got me making those impossible choices again, haven't you?' she said resentfully. 'A yes means that I'm feeble enough to be frightened merely because I'm standing on a precipitous slope with a landslide and a cascading river on one side and you—a possible sex-maniac—on the other; a no means you'll do something dire to test my courage to the limit.' He was laughing at her, she thought angrily. *At*, not *with*. 'I'm hungry. I want my lunch. Can we stop playing your version of Frighten the Maiden and go somewhere, anywhere, to eat?'

'Hang on to me. This is going to be exciting,' he said, his eyes dancing.

And she thought so too, heaven help her; she wanted to laugh, to let her eyes dance too. So she cast them down as if irritated, but somehow she sensed that he was well aware of the fact that she felt totally energised: by the adventure, by the slight danger, by him.

'A stroll, he said,' she muttered, pretending to be annoyed.

'You can't blame me for the landslide,' he told her in amusement. 'Now we have to get over the water. I'm going to jump first, and then you. It's not far, and I'll catch you.'

It looked easy, the way he effortlessly cleared the cascade of water and landed on a small hump of firm ground. Ellen tentatively let go of the small sapling and estimated the distance to be jumped. Offering up a small prayer to the fates, she flung herself across.

'Ahh!' Too late, she realised she'd misjudged and was going to fall short.

'Ellen. . .! Hell!' exclaimed Addan, looking concerned.

The icy water splashed up into her face as her feet sank into the soft ground and she flung herself out full-length in an effort to save herself from being swept off her feet, plunging her arms frantically into the foaming torrent for something to grab and trying to keep her body above the water. Her fingers touched the roots of a tree and she hung on grimly, her legs soaked and apparently incapable of moving an inch.

'I — I — !' The cold had taken her breath away.

'My hand,' said Addan urgently. 'You're quite safe. Let go of the tree. I'm here.'

'I — !'

'*Trust* me!' he roared.

Gingerly she stood up, ankle-deep in the freezing water, her hand stretching out to his. He gave an almighty heave, virtually dragging her across the loose soil to the safety of a huge pine. Safely lodged into Addan, who was braced against its trunk, she looked ruefully at her soaking legs, covered in thick red mud.

'Look at me!' she squeaked.

'Poor Ellen.' He pulled her to him in comfort, tucking her head into his chest. Her shoulders began to heave up and down. 'I'm sorry,' he crooned, rocking her as her chest joined in. 'You're too much of a city girl for this kind of thing. It's awful, I know. Wet and cold and filthy, miles from anywhere. I should never have brought you. You must hate this island. . .' His soothing voice faded. 'Ellen? Ellen?' he said suspiciously. 'What. . .?' His hands forced her head up and his look of astonishment made her bottled-up laughter burst out loud. 'You weren't crying!' he said indignantly.

'No!' she said, choking with her own laughter, the tears streaming down her cheeks. 'Oh, I think I'm getting hysterical! It — was — so — funny!' she jerked.

'Funny?' he scowled. 'What — — ?'

'Me,' she giggled. 'You, this. . .this mad scenario! It's crazy! I was going to lie in a darkened room for a few days and instead here I am, stuck on some isolated hillside behaving like a mountain goat with three legs and arthritis!'

Addan began to laugh too. 'I thought. . .' He shook his head in bewilderment. 'I'm amazed. You're not upset at all?'

She took a handkerchief from her pocket and wiped her eyes. 'No, only hungry.' Her beaming smile apparently quite disconcerted him.

'She falls in a mountain stream, gets plastered with mud and she's hungry!' he marvelled. 'I would have thought something like that would have turned you right off.' His brows met in a frowning V. 'You're a real bundle of surprises, Ellen,' he said slowly.

'That's me!' she said chirpily.

His hand pushed back a wet lock of hair from her forehead. 'What was that about a darkened room?' he murmured.

Ellen's brain sprang into alertness. 'Oh, recovering, you know.' She smiled prettily. 'Beauty sleep. All those parties catch up on you after a while.' She thought she sounded convincing and his prejudices about her did the rest. When he nodded with faint disapproval, she did her pretty smile again and felt secretly smug to be fooling her astute brother-in-law so successfully again.

'OK,' she said cheerfully, 'we've done the assault course and I reckon I got five for achievement and ten for effort. What's next?'

There was a faint narrowing of Addan's eyes and then they became unreadable. 'What would you like?' he asked with interest. 'There's the Wall of Death, hang-gliding from a peak or seeing who can roll to the bottom with the most bones intact.'

'I'll settle for getting back on the path and lunch,' she said ruefully.

'Suits me. Suits me fine,' he murmured, his eyes lowered. 'Oh, Ellen! You're very wet.' He bent and felt the fabric of her trousers. Ellen swallowed at the sight of his dark head and the view of black crescent lashes sweeping his strong cheekbones. Her hand lifted to touch his hair and she snatched it back again quickly. Just as well, because he looked up almost immediately. 'I think you ought to take those off,' he said, a wolfish grin on his face.

'I bet you do,' she said sardonically. 'But I'm going to stay decently covered while you're around. Pneumonia is marginally preferable to having you leering at my legs.'

The way Addan stood up made her muscles contract. One hand on her calf, one on her thigh. Her other thigh. A handful of buttock. His head came level with her breasts and he paused.

'Taking a breather,' he explained heavily. His innocent face rose slowly, inches from her body and then he grinned crookedly at her as if he'd got the better of her.

'If we weren't in danger of our lives from a hasty movement in any direction,' she said evenly, mastering the destructive curls of pleasure inside her, 'you would have had your face very thoroughly slapped.'

'I do take advantage, don't I?' he sighed. 'Turn around. I'll shove you uphill.'

'We'll go hand in hand,' she said sweetly. 'Then if I fall, so do you. And I'm certainly not suffering your hands on my rear again.'

'Come on, then, Mother Courage,' he laughed. 'I promise to be terribly well-behaved. God,' he groaned, 'how incredibly dull!'

Ellen primmed her rebellious mouth that wanted to smile and thrust out her hand. Addan caught it, kissed it and gave it a squeeze before shepherding her back up to the path as if she was something precious to him.

Squelching along in her saturated trainers, feeling extraordinarily cheerful, she noticed that the trees were thinning out and the views were becoming quite stunning, a vista around every corner where the *levada* hugged the twists and turns of the mountain.

It meant that the path was more perilous than before, though. Apart from the soft green agapanthus clumps, there was very little ground between her and a long, long drop. Holding her breath, she walked with great care and even greater concentration, one step at a time, determined not to be beaten.

To her relief, it wasn't long before they came to a spur of land jutting out by the path and Addan led her to sit beneath the small grove of contorted pines.

Here, she eased off her shoes and socks and used his handkerchief to dry her feet, refusing his offer to do that for her. Addan hung up her socks and tied her trainers to the lower branch of the tree in the sunshine. Then he carried the rucksack to the *levada* and extracted a bottle of Sercial, lowering it into the water.

He looked back at her. 'I'd better make sure this doesn't get swept back to the village,' he said, tying the bottle into place with the cords of his rucksack.

'You've done that before,' she smiled.

'Hundreds of times. Have a devilled crab sandwich.'

In the middle of wondering whether women had accompanied him on all these 'hundreds of times' and if they'd minded plunging across landslides, she looked at the package he offered her in surprise.

She opened the soft linen, thinking he'd been joking, but there they were, crab sandwiches. . .and delicious! 'Oh, these are *gorgeous*!' she drooled after one ecstatic bite. 'What happened to my ham? And where did you get this wonderful bread?'

'Ham seemed rather boring. Thereza — the maid — took my Alfa Romeo into Funchal early this morning,' he said nonchalantly.

'The maid drove that fabulous car?' she gaped.

'She's a very good driver,' said Addan, apparently not understanding the reason for her surprise.

Ellen reviewed her opinion of him. She'd always believed that he was a dyed-in-the-wool aristocrat who made sure servants knew their place, not a man who shared his car quite impartially.

'What else is there?' she asked, seeing him open another beautifully wrapped bundle.

'Madeira cake. One of hers,' he said, showing her the rich, dark cake inside. 'I promised you a taste of the real Madeira!' he smiled. 'It's got everything in it that's rich and spicy — especially black molasses. It keeps from one year to the next, they say.'

Her eyes danced. 'Do you ever give it a chance to prove the theory?'

He sighed. 'I have a sweet tooth,' he admitted, his eyes lingering on her mouth.

'What else has she packed?' asked Ellen a little breathily.

'There's a couple of chicken legs, bacon rolls stuffed with olives and some fancy hand-made chocolates. And some fruit. I hope you have an appetite.'

'Watch,' she laughed. 'It's wonderful, Addan.' She decided that was enough praise for him and tucked in. Of course, he'd honed his picnics to a fine art by now, choosing everything that would appeal to a female companion. Her mouth became wry as she scanned the convenient plateau and wondered how many of his women had lain here beneath him, enjoying. . .

Fiercely she bit into the fresh sandwich, vowing that he wouldn't get her rolling on the ground with him in any circumstances. For courage, she drank some more Madeira and felt the warmth hit her stomach.

He let out a contented sigh, leaning back against a tree on the edge of the spur and gazing out at the mimosa-covered hillside opposite. Far to the left was the deep blue sheet of the sea, the sun glinting so brilliantly there that it hurt to look at it.

'One of my favourite places on the whole island,' he mused quietly. 'And there's some stiff competition, I can tell you.'

'You must prefer Rio,' she probed.

'No.' His eyes flicked over to her and then he chewed reflectively on a chicken leg. 'Madeira. However, I thought it unwise to hang around here.'

'Oh. The married woman,' she said unhappily.

'Sort of.'

For a long while she ate and studied his absorbed face as he gazed ahead, scanning the snow-capped mountain peaks of a distant range beyond the valley. Slowly his eyes drifted over the nearer slopes, the sea of billowing yellow, the crags and pines, then the chestnuts and groves of blossoming cherry trees further down.

Lost in the contemplation of the incomparable beauty spread before him, he hardly touched his food and she was forgotten, though she felt no indignation or resentment. How could she? He'd come home after years of self-denial to the place he loved most: that was apparent in the way he leaned — almost like an eager lover — towards the breathtaking vista.

Ellen's heart beat faster at his yearning expression as he greedily recorded everything on his mind. She remained very quiet, surprised that such a forceful, dynamic man should allow her to see this side of himself; a man who appreciated the glory of nature as she did. Somehow that made him more human in her eyes and she found herself smiling gently.

Addan shut his eyes in blissful rapture, yet she was aware of a tension within him as if he was listening to every note of the molten birdsong that soared up from the thick forests below. His face lifted slightly, in

response to the same perfumed breeze that had tanta-
lised her nostrils.

An overwhelming feeling of tenderness came over
her. It was then that he turned and looked at her with
such burning eyes that she was caught unawares. She'd
expected gentleness — a dreaminess even. She got a
white-hot heat instead.

When he rose, she shrank back a little, his body
looking unnervingly menacing as if he'd been thinking
other thoughts than those concerning the pleasure of
beautiful scenery. But he went to the pile of fruit,
temptingly laid out on the napkin beside her, and
selected a mango.

'Most women would have interrupted my reminiscences,' he said huskily, his eyes dark and unfathom-
able. His fingers lightly touched her sleeve. 'I ignored
you. It was unforgivable to treat a woman with such
cavalier disregard. I must make amends.'

Ellen wanted to move away from him and the scary,
threatening air that surrounded his tense body. 'I've
been perfectly content, eating away here,' she said
nervously.

His fingers were busy peeling the mango. He lifted
the lush fruit to his mouth and bit into the juicy flesh,
his eloquent eyes never leaving her face for an instant.
The space between them suddenly seemed unendur-
able. With a slow, steady movement, he devoured the
fruit, holding her huge blue eyes hypnotically. When he
threw the stone into the abyss and began to lick his
fingers with deep concentration, she felt a warm weakness steal over her body.

He held out a mango in a gesture that was almost a
challenge.

'No. . .' She cleared her husky throat without much
success and saw a smile come to his juice-covered lips
like that on the face of a sphinx. 'No, thank you,' she
forced out hoarsely.

'It's good. Taste.'

And she did, by being gathered hungrily to him and

having her lips crushed against his, sweet, sticky, encouraging her tongue to dart out and savour before she knew what she was doing.

'Oh, no, Addan!' she croaked, half into his opening mouth.

Their tongues meshed. Ellen gave a long, shuddering groan, echoed by a growl deep in Addan's throat. His exploring mouth weakened her further, her languid arms floating up aimlessly to his head where her fingers toyed with the silken strands of his thickly waving hair.

She felt his weight pushing her thickly down, his mouth forcing her to yield to him in its voracious journey over her face, her neck, her shoulder—where he had wrenched her zipped top to one side in a savage movement that simultaneously thrilled and terrified her. He seemed desperate to kiss her, driven to a frenzy by the prospect of touching her body. The woman in her felt flattered. Her instinct for self-protection made her want to fight.

# CHAPTER SEVEN

'BEAUTIFUL,' he growled. 'The skin of a woman. Nectar of the gods.'

'If you're hungry ——' she began in desperation.

His dark, menacing face appeared above her. 'Hungry?' he muttered. 'My God!' he whispered harshly, his glittering hot eyes betraying the violence inside him. 'You've no idea how hungry I am!'

Her protest was stopped by his brutal mouth driving into hers in a rough, bruising kiss that left her gasping and helpless, the thudding urgency of her body filling her with shame. She wanted him as much as he wanted her.

His marauding fingers distracted her as they forced open her zip, exposing her thin T-shirt beneath. And then there was nothing to cover her, only his warm, firm hands, cupping her naked breasts with such fervour that her whole body arched in anguished longing.

Whatever he felt, she felt it too.

'First the wine, now taste the man,' he growled.

'Oh, please!' she begged in panic. She froze, mesmerised by the indolent sensuality of his smoke-dark eyes as they viewed the swelling flesh cradled in his hands.

'First, observe,' he whispered. Ellen quivered with tension. His gaze flowed over her breasts and as it did she felt them rise to his fingers, lifting wantonly, the skin shimmering in the sunlight. 'White gold,' he pronounced softly. Each forefinger hovered over a rosy nipple. 'And rubies. Second, inhale.'

'Addan ——!'

Like a hot sirocco, his breath skimmed over the surface of her skin, electrifying each hair, and then he inhaled, his nostrils curling in pleasure.

'Third,' he murmured, a wickedly seductive smile

curving his expressive mouth, 'a little movement. . .intensifies. . .'

'No, no, no!' protested Ellen, so tied up in the sensual web he'd spun that her words emerged as a husky croak and her hands merely fluttered in a vain attempt to break the spell he was weaving over her. For he lazily rotated his hard palms and she felt the peaks of her breasts thrust shamelessly against them.

'Fourth——'

She was there ahead of him. Taste. 'Oh, no,' she rasped. 'Leave me alone! I——'

Addan merely lifted a hand and pushed her chin back, reclaiming her lips, his eyes smouldering with intense lights, promising unknown delights which she had longed for since he had first kissed her when she was seventeen and which Bruno had never sated. This wasn't her, she thought, sinking beneath his kiss in helpless pleasure. It was a woman who'd been denied sexual release for too long. And now Addan, of all people, was offering her satisfaction. And she wanted it. Badly.

'That's right,' he said thickly. 'Surrender. Lie back and enjoy.'

Her eyes widened. Mutely she stared back into the merciless black eyes as his fingers brushed the peaks of her breasts. Although she barely moved in response, she knew he'd seen the flinch in her eyes and felt the split-second contraction of her loins as the spasms of pleasure flashed through her body.

'I won't enjoy this,' she whispered through softly pouting lips.

Addan raised a mocking eyebrow and gently teased her incredibly sensitised nipples. Steeling herself against any reaction, she forced back an instinctive, animal cry and held his gaze steadily. But her defiance didn't shame him. His expression became sensual, and drowsy, the heat of his body more intense, the movement of his fingers more rhythmical, more impossible to deny.

'God, you are lovely!' he growled. 'So. . .the tasting.'

His mouth surrounded one nipple and she waited in breathless anticipation for the warm, soft circle to close in and tug. He was very still, breathing heavily against her swollen breast, his body taut as a bow-string. It was hard, not crying out, not begging him to satisfy her craving. She struggled with her conscience, with her desperate frustration, and began to lose the battle. His eyes flicked up to hers; saw her half-closed lids, her pleading expression, and, with a savage groan, he pushed her nipple deep into his mouth and drew on it strongly.

'Oh, oh, oh!' she moaned softly. 'Addan, I ——'

'Sweetness, richness, honey, fragrant, mellow, full-bodied and so intoxicating that ——'

'Don't!' she shuddered, driven half crazy by his sensual litany.

'It's true. You affect me more than a wine. You want me. I want you,' he said, pausing briefly.

Ellen blinked at his ruthless logic and looked down at him, intending to deny her need. His tongue came out and licked the tip of her shamefully elongated breast that sprang thick and dark against his lower lip.

She let out her breath in a long, shuddering rush of air. Addan's lips burned their desire around the swell of each breast, his hands easing her top away. Ellen struggled feebly, her body languid and lethargic under his impassioned onslaught, and because she knew she wanted him with a madness that totally obliterated any wisdom or self-respect she'd once harboured.

Her hands drew his head up because she was unable to bear the feel of his mouth on her naked flesh any longer. She had to clear her head. Somehow.

But he had other ideas. In a swift movement, his hands had slid downwards, over the curve of her smooth stomach, and at the same time her gasp of shock was stifled by his violently sexual kiss as his tongue thrust hotly into the moist recesses of her mouth. Ellen's loins contracted at the wicked expertise of his stroking fingers moving with a heart-stopping rhythm, that vibrated deep into her body.

She was helpless, lost, swirling in a desire so powerful that it was as if he'd thrown her into a torrent and she'd never learnt to swim. Nothing had prepared her for the sensations claiming her body. Not the provocative movements he was so much a master of, not the effect his ragged breathing was having on her, not the blood roaring in her head nor the sensual languor of her limbs.

'Easy,' he murmured, when she bucked beneath him and moaned. His passion-drugged eyes gazed down at her. His pupils were enlarged, the thrust of his lip infinitely seductive. She forced his head towards her and their mouths met in a hard, desperate kiss, as if both of them had been denied satisfaction for too long. 'I've waited. . .for years,' he whispered.

The rhythms of her body took over. She moaned and sighed as his kisses exploded in a storm of passion till it seemed every inch of her body—naked, how had that happened? she thought hazily—had been caressed and covered, touched, nuzzled. . .

Every inch. All of it brought to life by his hands, his mouth, his teeth, by the mumbled words of desire that stirred her body into a raging need till she was fighting with him, crying out her demands.

'Kiss me, kiss me!' she moaned. 'There. Oh, Addan! I've never—oh, yes, there!' she sobbed, half delirious with wanton abandon.

He lay naked against her now, hard and demanding, the full power of his manhood both alarming and desirable. She felt herself being lifted to a sitting position and tucked on to his lap. Her soft breasts flowed against his muscular chest, the heavily laden peaks brushing the dark hairs in a delicate torture that made her throw back her head in pleasure.

His lips smouldered on her vulnerable throat, his hands rubbing her buttocks till she could bear it no longer. But she couldn't ask for what she wanted. So she moved, wriggling against his hard, velvety heat, her head spinning dizzily with hunger.

Gently, with a movement so infinitely slow that she groaned in frustration, he lifted her, just a centimetre. And brought her down again. Her anguished eyes met his.

'I want. . .' She could say no more, stunned into silence by the intense passion on his face.

He made the movement again and she felt the leap of violent arousal against her pelvis. He wanted her badly. He was teasing her, she thought wildly, delaying the moment she longed for.

'Say you want me,' he said fiercely.

She bit her lip, not daring to. His hands wrought magic with her body, taunting, teasing, his long fingers lighting an unquenchable fire. She could feel the liquid in her body, the violent beating of her heart against his chest, the hard, hard swell of her drum-tight breasts.

'Say it!' he growled.

Ellen shook her head dumbly, shuddering slowly at the intoxicating lift and fall of her body against his throbbing, quivering heat. Fire and flames seemed to be consuming her mind, and she could no longer think straight, not with Addan's sensual mouth doing such terrible, wonderful things to her.

He slid away and laid her down, his knee parting her legs before she could clamp them together. Her arms weakly invited him, and she lay there panting softly, silently and urgently pleading with him to make love to her, yet unable to speak the words aloud.

He smiled tenderly and her heart lurched. And for the first time, gazing at his infinitely desirable face, she realised why she had allowed him to go so far.

'Oh, God!' she whispered, her eyes closing in immediate defeat. The feeling inside her, the ache in her heart, the deep, deep desire, had something to do with his electrifying skills, but more to do with the fact that she loved him—and always had. 'Addan!' she wailed, appalled at the mind-shattering discovery.

All this time, she'd loved her brother-in-law.

'Say it, say it, my darling,' he murmured passionately. 'Tell me you want me as much as I want you. Let me make love to you. I have to end this terrible hunger inside me if I'm ever to leave. Until I do, I can't ever go. You hold me a prisoner——'

'I? Hold you. . .?' Confused, incapable of thinking straight she tried to avoid his questing mouth.

So it moved downwards, drifting over her arching body, delighting in tracing a path further and further towards his goal. And Ellen was helpless to stop him. He was going. He'd leave after this, satisfied. While she. . .'Ohh!' she moaned, feeling a desperation beyond endurance. 'Oh, Addan, please, please, I need you, I need——'

Her voice became strangled with emotion. He had lifted himself above her, hovering, dark and so utterly desirable that she could hardly bear it. Pain and pleasure sliced through her heart. He'd take her and go. He'd have what he wanted and she'd have only a memory. But that was preferable to nothing.

'I'm strong, Ellen, I am used to denying myself, to holding back till the right moment,' he whispered. 'But I can't stand this any longer.' His voice had hardened to an intense and savage growl and she realised she'd driven him to the limits of his ruthless self-control. 'Yes or no!' he demanded. 'It's that simple!'

But he didn't leave it at that. If he had, she might have been strong and denied him. Merciless in getting what he wanted, he was kissing her with such tenderness and sweetness that she was totally captured by his restraint, trusting him to be gentle with her.

She smiled and his lips lifted from hers. Her hand caressed his cheek, traced the high arch of his mouth. She felt the leap of his body, the desperate shudder that went through him, and experienced a sense of exultation that she could cause that reaction. Her fingers ran over his massive shoulders to the straining biceps and her palms lay in awe on the hard, heaving chest.

Slowly her lashes lifted and she tried not to let her eyes betray how much she loved him. There was a heart-wrenching sweetness about his face that seemed to crack open her mind and turn her into a woman who cared nothing for the consequences of her action, only for what she needed now. 'Love me,' she whispered huskily. 'Love me with all your heart.'

A terrible violence leapt to his eyes. Afraid, she lifted her hands to push him away, but he roughly kicked her legs further apart with a flick of his foot and as the fear mounted inside her he suddenly thrust fiercely into her: scalding, shockingly hard and filling her aching emptiness with intense, searing movement.

'I'll have all of you,' he muttered savagely. 'I'll imprint a memory on your beautiful body that you'll never forget as long as you live!'

She drowned in an onslaught of wild kisses and she let herself go, incapable of holding back as he unleashed the full force of his sexuality on her and the spiralling sensations took over her body completely.

'Love me!' she demanded hoarsely, not even knowing she spoke.

'Till I drop,' he growled, stilling inside her. Denied what her body craved, she cried out to him and tried to repeat his rhythm, but he held her body in a grip of iron so that she couldn't wriggle. 'Look at me, Ellen. Look at me!'

'I—I——' she gasped, his teeth savaging her lower lip, and she opened her heavy-lidded eyes like a woman emerging reluctantly from a drugged sleep.

'Look at me. Watch me,' he demanded softly.

He began to move again. In awe, she watched his face, the flush of colour, the parted lips, the expression of bliss that half-broke her heart. 'I love you,' she moaned. 'I love you!'

An enraged groan tore from his lips and she felt as if everything was exploding inside her. . .

And a short while later Addan drove her to the edge of sanity again. And, as if he could never be satisfied, he coaxed and teased and played with her body once more after that till she was so deeply satisfied that she fell asleep in his arms with sheer exhaustion and contentment. He woke her, lifting her on to his lap and gently making love to her, taunting her lack of stamina till she laughed and twined her arms around him, determined to show him that she did still want him. And would do so till the end of time, she thought, as the now familiar, wonderful sensations began to chase through her receptive body.

She woke to find herself tucked up in the curl of Addan's body, sweat slicking her skin. She didn't want to move. Every part of her felt replete. Addan's lips touched her cheek. 'Oh!' She blushed and automatically covered her body with her hands. What would he think of her? she groaned inwardly. Embarrassment was written in every line of her face. 'You're awake! How long. . .?'

'I haven't slept.'

Her clouded eyes scanned his anxiously. She knew why he hadn't been able to sleep. It was because he realised she'd been a virgin. There would be the awful explanations, the terrible story, his contempt.

'I —— ' She tried to sound less husky, less like a siren. 'I don't know what —— '

'Don't give me that,' he drawled. 'You're quite a wanton underneath that composed exterior, aren't you?' His finger traced her pouting upper lip. 'Not that I'm complaining. I always knew you were intensely passionate. And I've wanted to arouse that passion every time we've met.'

'Bruno —— ' she began harshly, her eyes lowered to hide her distress.

'Tell me about him,' he said softly. 'Was it like that with him?'

He waited, but she remained silent, twisting her

hands unhappily because she'd betrayed Bruno with her body now, as well as with her mind and emotions. *I'm sorry, Bruno.* 'Secrets of the bedroom,' she managed lightly.

'I'm jealous,' he murmured, kissing the nape of her neck. 'I envy him for waking beside you every morning and taking you to bed every night.'

She wanted to tell him. But dared not trust him. What had happened between them had been lust on his part: an obsessive need to possess her. For some reason, he hadn't found her sexual inexperience a give-away: he thought she'd had a normal married life — and, of course, the fact that she'd been a virgin would never have occurred to him! Married women rarely were. . .

Ellen bit back a sob of self-pity. No wonder her marriage had failed. Bruno must have sensed what she never knew: that she'd loved his brother.

She shut out the past and turned her thoughts to protecting herself. A sophisticated woman would be casual about giving her body with such flagrant abandon. Casual, she thought. That's the way. Let him think I needed sexual gratification. Her tongue slicked over her lips in worry. Had she made herself vulnerable by showing him her real feelings? She couldn't remember — what she'd said aloud and to herself inside was muddled up together.

Boldly she placed her hand over his mouth. 'No recriminations, no explanations,' she husked, quivering as he kissed her fingers with an intense passion. 'But you realise it's been a long time for me.'

'That was evident,' he smiled. 'Are you very tired?'

Widening her eyes, she gasped at his insatiable sexual energy. 'Addan! You can't. . .!' Her voice trailed away in embarrassment.

'Not yet! I just wondered how you felt about wandering up to the waterfalls,' he laughed.

She wanted to hide — her face, her body, her whole

self. She wanted to curl up in a dark room and stay there till the shame of her surrender went away.

So she stretched and forced a smile. 'I think I want to go home,' she said huskily.

'Home.' His eyes flickered with sharp, flinty lights. 'Sure. We'll return another day.'

Never, she thought fervently. Never. The thought of passing — or pausing on — the site of her downfall was quite unthinkable.

Feeling drowsy and woolly-limbed, she was forced to let Addan help her to dress, to suffer his kisses and his flattery as he did so. What upset her most was the fact that she loved it, every minute of it, and she ended up clinging to him and kissing him back, touching his glorious dark hair in delight and trailing her fingers down the powerful cheekbones, marvelling at his flaw-less, satin skin.

Firmly he unwound her fingers, and she felt rebuked, as if she'd become something of a nuisance. 'The mists are coming down,' he said gently. 'I think we should start back.'

'Oh! Is there danger?' she asked anxiously, seeing a thick blanket of white cutting off the tops of the peaks.

'Of getting wet, that's all!' he grinned.

'Oh, I don't mind a bit of rain,' she said absently.

'You surprise me,' he murmured, his eyes shrewd. 'But I think you'll get more than a bit of rain. We must try to get over the landslip before the weather comes in. That's the only part where it might be difficult.'

The thunder began to roll around the mountains, bouncing off the rock walls in a deafening roar.

'Sounds as if someone's bellowing into a bucket,' cried Ellen, as she hurried along the narrow path, quite easily crossing the narrow part as if she'd never feared heights in her life.

'Not afraid, are you?' he called, turning back to her.

'Thunder always excites me!' Her gaze faltered. He looked annoyed.

'We'll be all right, providing the lightning doesn't bring down any trees,' he said laconically.

'That's right,' she answered with a wry smile, 'think positive.'

Addan's mouth twitched and he moved on ahead. Spots of rain began to patter on her face and he pulled out their waterproofs. 'We're going to get soaked.'

'I'm drip-dry.'

Ellen tried to work out why the storm pleased her. Perhaps it was because it took her mind off what she'd been doing. It gave her something else to think about and made that gap between those unreal moments of frenzied passion and normal life a little less difficult to bridge. They were doing something ordinary again and Addan had been diverted from her unconditional surrender.

She lifted her face to the rain and let it cleanse her face. It began to get cold and she shivered, feeling the first dampness penetrating her back. That was what came of Bruno's maid throwing the waterproof into the washing! she thought ruefully, as they came to the landslide.

'You're like a bedraggled rat.'

Her peal of laughter echoed around the mountains. 'I am, aren't I?' She grinned happily, placing her hands on Addan's shoulders and letting him swing her down. he hugged her briefly, his face showing a puzzled amusement.

Keep him guessing, she told herself. Stay a mystery. She'd be safe if he never found his way to her vulnerable soft centre. So far her role as a shallow, partying gold-digger, with nothing in her head but mushy peas, had been a bit patchy. She must step up her defences and keep her feelings forever a secret.

'Take care now,' he warned, as she prepared to jump across the foaming river where she'd come to grief before.

'I will,' she answered with unusual vehemence. 'I mean to. Though if I miss this time it'll hardly matter —

I'm soaked to the skin anyway. I might as well walk through the darn river and be done with it!'

'Poor Ellen,' he said silkily. 'A far cry from the glitz and glamour of your preferred life, isn't it?'

She paused, alerted by his tone — cunning, that was it. Well, she could be cunning too. 'I'm going to make you take me to all the best shops in Funchal tomorrow,' she said, managing not to grimace at the thought. She'd shopped enough in the last few years. 'And you can buy me a present. Then you can treat me to a gorgeous meal somewhere very, very expensive.'

The scorn on his face cut through her like a knife. 'It's a deal,' he murmured, his eyes gleaming. 'Small price to pay for what I've been given.'

Men! she thought angrily. Some of them never saw beyond the crass level of purchasing women and paying a price for sexual favours. It sickened her that Addan was in that league.

She tilted her head haughtily, tensed, and jumped, soaring right across the water. Instantly she was gathered into his arms and he kissed her wet face inch by dripping inch before letting her go and clambering up to the path. Despite her irritation with him, he'd left her behind, panting and miserable because she wanted him to stay with her and solicitously to help her up as if he adored her.

Women! she thought, with even greater exasperation. Strong and weak, reduced as she'd been to feebleness by a man's mouth!

Lightning forked in a blinding flash and a tremendous roll of thunder racketed around the mountains. With a small yelp of surprise, she scrambled up to the path like a goat. Baffled, she saw genuine concern on Addan's face.

'Two presents,' she said sharply, to stifle the upswell of tenderness she felt for him. How *could* she have these emotions? she asked herself impatiently.

He scowled and jerked her towards him roughly, his brutal mouth forcing down on hers in a possessive, angry kiss. 'This is how I like my women,' he said savagely. 'Heartless, giving me no emotional hassle at all. And sexy. Very sexy.' A ruthless hand pushed beneath her clothes and massaged her tender breast.

The lethargy stole over her body like a flowing river and she shamelessly leaned into him, her hands trying to open his waterproof jacket before she knew what she was doing. With a sardonic lift of his eyebrows, he pushed her away and she felt a sick sensation in her stomach that he'd so easily shown that he could do anything he wanted with her.

*Hate me*, she begged with her eyes, the rain falling on her upturned face unheeded. And leave me alone. 'I learnt long ago to let my head rule my heart,' she said in a hard tone, desperate to escape the domination he wielded over her. She'd do anything, say anything to be free of her love for him. 'Emotions get in the way of ambition.' As soon as she'd said the words, she hated herself.

'You are a selfish little bitch, aren't you?' he murmured.

'You think that and we'll get along fine,' she said with a light laugh, and loathed herself even more.

But as they walked back beneath the gnarled tamarisk trees, the rain shimmering in tiny diamond drops on the ferny foliage, she felt she was winning a hollow victory. In her heart of hearts, she wanted Addan to respect and to love her. It was ironic that she had been forced into the situation where she must make him despise her.

She scuffed at the wet burgundy soil crossly and came to a dead stop, her head lifting in sudden awareness. How stupid she was! She'd got it wrong! *Why* did she have to keep pretending? Hadn't she spent the last five years living a lie, and hadn't she vowed that her life here in Madeira would be free of all artifice?

Thoughtfully Ellen sat on the edge of the swollen *levada* and watched its dark waters speeding on their way down to the village. Addan had turned a corner ahead and she was left to gaze out at the still, silent valley, now wreathed in mysterious mists.

She was what she was. Addan would have to take her at face value. He could have her love — and when he left, as he inevitably would, it would hurt her, but at least she'd know that she'd been true to herself, instead of indulging in this eternal male-female game-playing that made a mockery of honest emotions. It sickened her and always had.

She wanted to be free from loving him, but what was the point of trying to go against her nature? Perhaps the more she knew him, the less she'd love him. His awful condescension, for instance.

Ellen's eyes were thoughtful. It had been Bruno who'd made her aware of Addan's extraordinary qualities, grumbling about his brother's power over women and his astonishing success in handling one business crisis after another.

All through her marriage it had been 'Addan this' and 'Addan that' till she'd felt she knew the man better than her own husband. Bruno had appeared to think that his brother could dance any opposition off the floor, win *Mastermind* and persuade crotchety grandmothers to take up karate. She was probably in love with a myth that didn't even exist, and since she was going to get hurt anyway she might as well stop acting against her own desires and come clean.

He was afraid of women's love. Her eyes gleamed. Hard luck! She'd live for each day, love each day, enjoy her time with him. . .till it ended. Too much of her life had been wasted already on false pretences. This would be the real thing, however short. It was time she had a ball!

'Ellen! Ellen! What the hell are you doing? I thought you'd fallen off the mountain!'

Jumping up, she ran to the frowning Addan and impulsively hugged him, dislodging a shower of raindrops from his wet hair. For a moment she thought he responded with surprised warmth, and then he pushed her back, his expression unreadable.

'Sorry!' she said happily. 'I was doing a bit of dreaming and thinking back there.'

'About what?' he asked warily.

'You and me,' she said, bursting with her new frankness.

'And?'

Her arms wrapped around his neck and he remained very stiff, looking down at her as if she were an irritating child. 'I've decided to enjoy you,' she said, brushing water from his dark eyebrows, her eyes laughing.

'God help me!' he muttered.

Yet his kiss was tender, whatever his air of alarm; sweet and longing, mingled with the soft rain. Ellen had the feeling that his stony heart had been touched by her honesty. Then his next words disappointed her.

'You know I can't keep my hands off you,' he growled. 'Don't ask me why——'

'You're a very sensual man,' she said huskily, nuzzling his chin. 'Women arouse you. I understand that.'

'Please, the last thing I want is an understanding woman,' he drawled, making her laugh. And there was the glimmer of a smile touching his mobile mouth, too. 'You're far more shrewd than I ever imagined,' he murmured. 'I can see you're going to extract all you can from me in return for satisfying my lust. All right. I can afford you well enough.' His eyes blazed with a sudden intensity. 'But,' he said grimly, with an air of male possession, his fingers closing on her jaw, 'expect to deliver the goods whenever and wherever I want. OK?'

Abruptly released, Ellen flinched at his arrogant demand. 'Within reason,' she said quietly.

'No, Ellen,' he muttered. 'There's no reason about this, not for me, anyway. I'm acting from pure, primitive instinct. Heaven help us both.'

The rain began to fall in torrents and they ran, Ellen

astonishing herself at her own sure-footedness on the narrow path. It was exhilarating and they arrived back at the car warm, tingling, and panting heavily.

'Take your waterproof off and then leap in,' yelled Addan above the downpour, holding open the passenger door for her. 'Quick!'

'Geronimo!' she yelled in elation, hurling herself into the car.

'Geronimo again!' he laughed, flinging himself in beside her, his face streaming with water. 'Now, let's have a look at you. You're wet through! Here. Let's put the heater on. Take those shoes and socks off.'

'Yes, sir,' she grinned. 'Isn't this fun?'

Bent over her knee as he helped her to unlace her soggy trainers, he glanced up at her in astonishment. Then he smiled. 'Yes,' he said with a small chuckle. 'It is.' She placed a hand on his dripping hair and stroked it happily. 'There you go,' he said gruffly, easing the shoes off.

'Ugh!' She shrugged her clammy spine away from the wetness of her top. 'Trust you to be entirely dry,' she said ruefully.

'You'd better not take that off. Let it dry on you,' he frowned. 'Have some food and a warm drink. I don't want you getting ill.'

'That's nice,' she smiled. 'Oh, my life! Look at my hair, my face. . .!'

She leaned her head back and tried to squeeze out some of the water. Addan kissed her throat and then shrugged off his jumper, rough-towelling her hair with it before he tackled his own. And afterwards she felt beautifully cherished from his fussing, and they drove off, both in high spirits.

On the long journey back, they played a silly game of 'I Spy', with Addan insisting that every word should begin with the letter L. So she mischievously offered L.C. for 'low cloud' — which he astutely guessed after some hilarious suggestions, and he retaliated with a vengeance.

'L.L.C.,' he said smugly as they drove past a small village.

'Lifting low cloud?' she tried.

'No.'

'Last little cuddle?' She giggled wickedly.

He slanted dark eyes at her. 'I have plenty of those left. Give up?' She nodded. 'Long-legged chicken,' he said in triumph.

'I can't see it!' she protested

'I could, when I said, "I Spy",' he answered, unperturbed. 'I might bend the rules a little, but I do try to keep a vague hold on the truth.'

'Rotter!' she complained and her sharp mind wondered whether that went for everything he did.

'I'm curious,' he mused, his eyes shrewd as they rested on her tousled, steaming hair and stained clothes. 'Forgetting the mind-blowing sex for a moment — as if I could — have you enjoyed today? All of it?'

Her beaming smiled answered. 'Enormously,' she said happily.

'Hair mussed, no make-up, wet through, trailed along vertiginous paths and flung across landslides, half running through a downpour. . .? That doesn't sound like the female who shops till she drops. You know, you're almost like two different women.'

'You get more for your money with me,' she smiled.

A sigh of exasperation hissed from his lips. 'You're an intriguing little minx. You captivated Bruno and all his friends. You show no concern for the fact that you look —— '

'Like a drowned rat,' she provided, her eyes slanting to his.

'Correct,' he murmured drily. 'Perhaps you know you could look fabulous in sackcloth and ashes. You've got that glow about you now —— '

'Walking. The warmth in here. The wine,' she began.

'And sex,' he said bluntly.

Her frank eyes met his again. 'Yes,' she husked.

The black eyes melted as if his body was as liquid as hers. 'You do seem happy,' he said quietly.

'I am.' She left it at that.

'You have all you want.' His voice was softly seductive.

'I suppose I do,' she admitted. The idea sank in and she turned a joyful face to him. 'I have!' she cried in delight.

His hand brushed her face briefly and then he concentrated on the road again, peering intently through the sweeping rain. 'So easy to please,' he drawled. 'How lucky you are.'

'What do *you* want, then?' she asked, fascinated.

She saw the strong jaw clench and a hardness replace his amusement with her. 'I want to be dry,' he drawled and she had to be content with that and just laugh, instead of probing for his inner secrets.

She lay in her marble bath, surrounded by bubbles, her skin pink from the warm, sensual water. Music played: a heart-rending song that seemed to speak of poignant love-affairs and the pain of human tragedy.

Lifting her slender shoulders slightly, Ellen renewed her vow to live for the moment. Happiness now. Pain later. It was worth it; she needed so desperately to be with Addan. The time spent with him in the car had been precious; moments of easy companionship and much laughter. It was more than she'd ever had before.

'This is *fado*. Like it?'

Her head jerked around, the curls piled on top of her head tumbling over one eye. 'Don't I get any privacy?' she murmured, her insides turning over at the sight of Addan's glorious naked body.

'No.' He put down the bottle of champagne and two glasses and tucked her hair back into the ridiculously large bow she'd tied her hair with and calmly stepped into her bath. '*Fado*' he said, for all the world as though they were discussing the financial situation on a train to the City, 'is our national song.' His dark, smudgy eyes mocked her. 'Gets you here, doesn't it?' he said, pressing a hand to his big chest.

His legs slid further alongside her thighs and she busied herself with soaping her arms and inspecting her fingernails till her heart beat slowed down.

'Don't kid yourself,' she said quietly. 'You know it tears at your emotions, just as it does mine.'

'Damn you,' he said softly, suddenly quite still. 'Damn you for being. . .' Addan bit back the words he'd been going to say. 'For being so contrary and female,' he said and reached down for the champagne, handing her a fizzing glass.

Hugging herself with delight, she lifted it to him. She was getting to him!' 'Salude,' she smiled, not needing the champagne to feel bubbly inside. 'Am I discovering a human heart inside that impenetrable chest of yours? Has it replaced the mechanical steam-hammer?'

He eyed her cynically over the thin rim of the crystal glass. 'Don't imagine for one moment, Ellen,' he said softly, 'that you're going to twist me around your little finger. I am a very different man from the ones you've known before.' The half-smile vanished. 'Get out,' he ordered, jerking his head with an air of quiet authority.

'What?' she cried with indignation.

'Out!' he snarled suddenly. 'Or I'll lift you myself!'

'But——!' Seeing the angry rise of his shoulders, she stood up quickly and stepped on to the black marble floor, the bubbles fizzing on her body. 'Why are you playing the heavy?' she complained, taking a nervous step back as he climbed out too and walked menacingly towards her.

A huge soft white towel was wrapped around her. 'Dry me!' he said curtly.

She opened her mouth to protest and gasped at the crackle of anger in his dark eyes. 'Addan——!'

'I collect, any time, any place,' he reminded her in a tone of barely controlled violence.

Like an automaton she began to dry his body, her hands shaking. Addan was proving to be as much of a mystery to her as she was to him. Her lower lip trembled. She was afraid of his anger.

'I'm not doing any more,' she said huskily, unable to bring herself to look, or to touch him below his waist.

With an impatient growl, Addan dragged the towel from her grasp and wrapped it around him then began to dry her body. Pinkly glowing, she set her teeth against the rhythmic sweeps of his hand.

And then he reached for the bottle of champagne and poured the remains of it over her shoulders, her breasts. . .

'Ohh!' she squealed, as the ice-cold liquid hit her flushed skin and flowed downwards. She stood there, startled, looking down at her tightening nipples and the gleaming golden rivulets that ran around the high globes of her breasts. Bubbles popped and fizzed on her skin, ticking each fine body hair and sensitising every inch of her body, outside and inside.

Without a word, Addan picked her up and carried her to the bedroom where he slid her to her feet and began to lick her dry.

# CHAPTER EIGHT

SEVERAL delirious hours later, they were friends again — friends, lovers, Ellen's head in such a wonderful whirl that she didn't know and hardly cared. Only that Addan had made love to her as she'd always wanted: like a man who cherished the very ground she walked on.

He was laughing at her now, at her inability to decide what to wear. 'Something fit for a siren,' he teased from where he lounged like a lord on her bed.

'I've got so much that answers that description,' she answered tartly.

'I'm sure you have,' he replied, amused.

Standing in midnight-blue satin underwear before the enormous antique linen-press, she frowned, not meaning to have given the wrong impression. It had been a joke, the kind of quip she might have made in the old days when she was a teenager. Yet he didn't look contemptuous. Only expectant.

Cheerfully he blew her a kiss and she turned back, trying to make a choice. Something that would make her utterly desirable. The sheath. She lifted it out and Addan whistled his approval.

'Black, slippery, touchable. Put it on then I can take it off,' he husked.

'Addan! I'm putting it on and it's staying on! Then I'll cook you something,' she reproved.

'No need. Thereza's left something for us,' he said indulgently. 'I didn't fancy your bread and ham.'

'Just as well. I'm a rotten cook,' she grinned, wriggling the skin-tight dress up her supple body and ignoring Addan's growl of admiration. Satisfied, she checked the lie of the strapless top in the mirror and her fingers stilled.

Even she, without vanity, could see why Addan was breathing so heavily. Her hair was still piled on top of her head, a few tendrils tumbling around her face. The dress hugged her curves in a series of hills and valleys, its gleaming surface inviting a man's exploratory touch. And so did her skin, warm gold and fired from inside with contentment and high-octane energy.

Her brilliant blue eyes sparkled back at her and as she clipped on the long cascading pearl earrings that hung to her collarbone she saw how the pearls lent a gently gleaming frame to the soft pink of her moist mouth.

In the mirror, she saw Addan come up behind her and stand a few inches away, looking at her reflection critically — but with no expression on his face that she could detect. Then his hand cupped the tight curve of her buttocks, swept around her hip and dipped into her waist. She tipped her head back and saw from under her lids that his face had become sultry, the black eyes smouldering with a thousand fires.

'Beautiful,' he whispered, his fingertips enjoying the feel of warm flesh beneath the sliding satin. For a brief second, his fingers paused on the deep cleft between her breasts and then ran along her collarbone to her shoulders. Which he kissed, one and then the other. 'And you will be mine,' he said and turned on his heel to walk out of the room.

Ellen gulped and let out the breath that had been building up inside her lungs. He had an obsession with mastering her. She met her own eyes in the mirror and saw the steel behind them. A smile softened her tense face and it became a broad grin.

'We'll make him accept me as his equal,' she whispered conspiratorially to her reflection. 'Before he leaves.' A shadow crossed her eyes but she refused to let it remain.

Curled up on the sofa later, Thereza's gourmet meal inside her, Ellen sighed with contentment. He'd appeared earlier in a dinner-jacket, the sharp white tailoring of the linen suit such a contrast with his strong, tanned face that she'd felt weak at the knees to look at him.

'You dazzle my eyes,' she'd smiled.

'I feed on yours,' he'd answered, and she'd shivered, knowing that even for him this was a special moment.

She'd stood on tiptoe to kiss him and the sweetness of his mouth had been undeniable. No harshness, no brutality. Just tender loving. It was there! she'd thought, her hopes rising. He could feel gentle emotions! Armed with that knowledge, she'd sparkled all evening and now was pleasantly relaxed.

The strains of a *fado* died away and neither of them stirred to replace the CD.

'How late it is!' she murmured lazily. 'It's been a perfect day,' she added. 'Dreamy. I seem to have been whisked from one world to another in a remarkably short space of time.'

'Sleep with me tonight,' murmured Addan in her ear. 'Come to bed with me now.'

How lovely. To wake up in his arms. . .'I'm terribly tired,' she told him gently, wondering if he was going to assert his rights.

'Just to sleep. I want you with me. Soft, warm. . . Ellen——' He hesitated.

'Mmm?' she breathed.

'You've enjoyed the day, you say. I still can't believe that. You've put up a good show of being amused by the problems that have beset us today——'

'Why did you choose that particular place to take me?' she asked, suddenly suspicious. He didn't answer and she demanded to know with her eyes.

'OK,' he admitted huskily. 'I wanted you off the island as soon as possible. I tried to make the day as unpleasant as possible for you.'

Her heart was beating hard. 'Why?'

'It's too easy to fall in love——' Ellen stopped breathing at Addan's hesitation. He pressed his warm lips on her forehead. 'To fall in love with Madeira,' he growled and she was left chiding herself for imagining for one second that he'd been close to an admission of temptation. 'You see, when I landed, I knew at once that I wanted to come back here to live. I didn't want you around. I thought you'd hate what I had in mind for you today and I'm intrigued that you didn't — or that you're pretending you didn't. What are you up to, little minx?' he murmured.

'You're intrigued? Oh, good!' she said smugly. Then, aware of his exasperation, she cuddled into his warm chest and took pity on him. 'I was afraid when we were driving along that road — and afraid of the heights. I suppose you hoped I'd run screaming from it all in terror,' she said ruefully. 'But in fact you did me a favour. No one had ever made me face up to my fears before and I feel stronger for doing so.'

'And the walk? Falling in the river and getting muddy?' he asked in amusement.

'I love walking,' she said happily. 'Always have. Bruno and I never. . .' She bit her lip at her momentary disloyalty. 'He wasn't keen,' she said. 'As for the rest, well, I've had years of dolling up in constricting clothes and being immaculately groomed every minute of the day and it was wonderful to get out into the fresh air and breathe freedom.'

'You should never have married him ' he muttered. She wanted to say that she knew that, but her pity and affection for Bruno prevented her. 'Tell me about him,' he persisted ruthlessly. 'Was he taking drugs? Were you?'

'Addan, I don't want to——' she began in a strained voice.

'He's — was — my brother,' he said tightly. 'I have to know.'

'All right.' She rose and walked over to the open window where the cool night air brought subtle scents of the outdoors into the darkened room. Her hand rested on the silk sheers, billowing in the breeze, and she lifted her face to the starry night sky, drawing in a long, steadying breath. 'When you came, the last time you saw him alive,' she said quietly, 'he was trying to appear normal. He didn't want you to know how ill he was.'

'For God's sake, why?' demanded Addan hoarsely.

She turned, a slim, sleek silhouette against the ivory curtain. 'He hated showing weakness in front of you,' she whispered, remembering Bruno's hysteria when he'd known his brother was visiting.

To hide their financial difficulties, Bruno had insisted on purchasing huge and vulgarly ostentatious plants to decorate the entrance of their villa in Nice. Gigantic floral displays in every room, including the bathroom. Champagne everywhere. House guests, to lounge around the pool in their exotic finery, and food of such lavish proportions that it had sickened her to look at it. And even now she couldn't tell Addan of this, because she'd promised she wouldn't.

'The drugs he took were muscle relaxants, to help his mobility,' she continued shakily. 'And I think he probably gulped down some "uppers", to keep up with your phenomenal energy.'

'And you?' Addan's face looked dark and bleak against the gleaming white of his dinner-jacket. Poor darling, she thought. This was hurting him.

'I've never taken pills. I was exhausted.' Her lips thinned. No way was she going to say why—that she'd struggled to understand their financial position and to run around cooking and cleaning and nursing the increasingly difficult Bruno.

'I'm not surprised, with all that endless partying,' Addan frowned. 'Why —— ?'

'Because he wanted it!' she cried wildly. 'I'm sorry, Addan,' she went on, more in control now that was out, 'but you have to understand that. I didn't want the parties. I didn't particularly want the kind of life we led. Bruno did. It gave him enjoyment. He'd never had it before, you see—he'd missed out on it because he was shy and if he went to a party with you then he suffered in your shadow. And who was I to deny him that when he — he —' a shuddering sob ran through her body ' — when he was dying?' she whispered.

Addan didn't move an eyelid. 'You never told me. You let me go back to Rio, hating you for involving him in such a shallow life and having had a violent row with my only brother for putting up with your whims and paying through the nose for the privilege of having a beautiful sex-kitten available.'

'I wanted him to tell you he had been given only six months to live,' she croaked, her eyes huge and swimming with tears. 'We had a row too! He didn't want you to know!'

'*Why*?'

Ellen shrank back as the word was flung at her, wrenched from the depths of Addan's body. An overwhelming sense of sadness and sympathy washed over her. He'd lost his brother and had never said goodbye.

'I don't want to hurt you,' she said hesitantly.

'It's hurting me more not to know.'

She nodded, understanding that. 'Like needing to know the end of a horror film.'

'Exactly,' he muttered. 'Exactly that.'

Slowly she crossed the heavy tapestry carpet, her heart going out to him. With a graceful movement, she sat at his feet and rested her slender arms on his knees, looking up at him with intense compassion. The sorrow in the lines of his face, the haunted darkness of his eyes, pained her deeply.

'He spoke of you almost constantly during our marriage,' she said quietly. 'It was a mixture of admiration, awe and resentment. According to him, you were invincible. You'd taken his girlfriends — ' He scowled and she waited for his comment.

'They fawned on me,' he growled. 'I didn't want them. I had women of my own.'

'Whatever the reason, they always abandoned Bruno,' she said gently. 'And he became scared of ever keeping a girl with you around. He had a terrible inferiority complex, Addan — and a guilt complex too, because he felt love for you but hated being constantly compared with you and never matching up.'

Addan stared into space, his hand absently stroking the nape of her neck. 'I knew that,' he said huskily. 'There wasn't anything I could do about it. I'd been thrown into a position at an early age where I had to fight or go under. I'm a fighter. I sense that you are too.' He smiled faintly at her and she answered with a tremulous smile of her own, loving him more than she ever had. 'Bruno. . . Ellen, you lived with him. You know what he was like. Full of wild ideas, incapable of recognising spongers and hangers-on. . .OK. I'll level with you. My opinion is that he was weak. I loved him dearly and he was my brother, but he needed protecting from himself.'

'Or gold-digging women.'

'Do you blame me for trying to frighten you off?' he asked quietly.

'No. Your method.'

He smiled ruefully. 'Bruno made it quite clear to me why he wanted you. I objected to that reason. Old-fashioned that I am,' he said wryly, 'I believe that marriage should be for love alone and I thought he'd probably find someone to love if he waited.'

Ellen stiffened. 'I thought ——'

'He didn't love you, Ellen, you must know that.'

'No! I don't! What did he tell you?' she asked, her mouth dry.

'That you were beautiful beyond belief, that you were a habitual liar and couldn't open your mouth without being deceitful. That you stumbled into his yacht, with some pretence that an intruder had tried to assault you ——'

'That was true!' she gasped, open-mouthed with shock. Bruno hadn't lied like that about her! He couldn't!

'He thought it was deliberate,' said Addan grimly, his eyes shuttered. 'Oh, it appealed to his protective instincts and he was flattered that a woman like you should choose him — and to go to the lengths of appearing in a skimpy bikini and allowing him to comfort you. But he knew what you were after.'

'Please, Addan!' she moaned faintly, appalled.

'He told me you were a bitch,' he went on relentlessly, his voice hardening, 'but that he wanted you as a prize to give him some standing in the eyes of other men. And your price was marriage.'

'It's not true!' she cried vehemently. 'None of it! He didn't say all that — you're lying! Addan,' she wailed, clawing at his thighs, 'tell me you're lying!'

'I swear by all that I hold dear that he told me this,' he said quietly.

She slumped to the ground in a boneless heap. Bruno. . . She'd given up her freedom, her self-respect and her independence to a man who wasn't worth — no! 'No!' she said aloud, shaking her head so that her silky hair flew in all directions. 'No!' she wailed, lifting her unhappy face to Addan. 'Why. . .?'

'God knows. Maybe he was afraid I'd. . . Perhaps he wanted to make sure I'd never touch you with a ten-foot bargepole. He knew I loathe grasping women. Didn't work, did it?' he said bitterly. 'I still couldn't keep my hands off you.'

'I didn't marry him for his money. I keep telling you,' she said tightly. 'I knew he wasn't hard up, obviously, but until you told me I was unaware of how rich he was.'

'So you loved him.'

'I——' Ellen bit her lip. Affection. Distress, after hearing Bruno's story about always losing his girlfriends to his brother. And when Bruno had heard of Addan's visit to Amsterdam, he'd threatened suicide if she didn't marry him. Her loving heart had felt such sympathy for his distress and guilt that she couldn't deny him and thought her sympathy was love. Wrong and stupid though she'd been, her motives were unselfish. 'No,' she whispered. 'I thought I did at first, I really did. He was so kind and I needed someone badly. He looked after me, paid me attention, listened, adored me.' Or she'd thought so at the time. Her hand clutched at her stomach where nausea swelled alarmingly. Bruno had trapped her in a loveless marriage merely to prove his worth to his brother. 'We talked a lot — well, he talked about you,' she amended huskily. 'He liked me to cheer him up and we went to parties —— '

'Ah. The parties.'

Her eyes pleaded with him. 'Addan, he'd never been invited before. He revelled in the novelty. He said that people asked me because I amused them, that I was a novelty with my lack of sophistication and the fact that I didn't care if I made social gaffes. He said they loved my cheerfulness and it lifted their boredom. He began to live for the first time —— '

'Through you.'

She hung her head. 'Yes. OK. Through me. But for him it was one step better than living in your shadow.'

'God! Who'd have a family?' growled Addan.

Ellen flinched. She would. She'd longed for one. Her hand faltered, close to his, and then closed over the big, worryingly cold fingers. 'I don't expect you to cast aside all your assumptions and prejudices immediately,' she said quietly. 'But will you reserve judgement? Give me an opportunity —— '

'To what?' he frowned. 'Capture me?' He leaned forward. 'What are you after, Ellen? Don't you have enough money of your own that you have to align yourself with me and get yourself a few more presents, a nice stack of money for your old age when you're no longer svelte and sexy and beautiful?'

Pain shone from her eyes. 'Don't, please don't,' she whispered. 'I like being with you — most of the time. I want you to drop the defences you've erected against me —— '

'I'm sure you do,' he murmured. 'But you're too late. You should have met me when I was ten. I think you might have wrought your magic on me then. Unfortunately for you — for any woman — I'm far too cynical and wary now to let any woman into my heart so that she can wreck my life.'

'Then I'll be satisfied with what we have,' she said huskily.

'Good. I'm glad we understand one another, Ellen. No complications, no emotional blackmail. No expectations of love or marriage.' His eyes gleamed. 'For that, I'm going to give you a really special present.'

'I don't want ——'

His hand covered her mouth and she glared at him mutinously over it. 'Take it,' he said laconically. 'I feel I owe you less that way.'

'You owe me nothing other than courtesy and respect,' she said proudly.

'Miracles, as you pointed out, take a little while,' he drawled. 'In the meantime, take what I offer you. Who knows? One day you could be left alone and in need.' That was highly likely, she thought morosely. 'I have a business,' he said softly, caressing her sullen face.

She lifted her chin, aroused immediately by his delicate touch. 'I don't want a business.'

He smiled. 'It rightly belonged to Bruno because it's based in Angola. It's a sisal plantation on the African coast. I think you ought to have it. I will gift it to you in the next few days. Don't worry,' he mocked, seeing her face. 'You'll get diamonds and designer clothes too.'

'What am I going to do with a sisal plantation?' she asked wryly. 'Do you want me to live in Africa as an overseer?'

'No,' he husked, tenderly kissing her. 'I want us to live here together.'

'You. . .want ——!'

'For the moment,' he whispered in the shell of her ear. 'Till I'm tired of you.'

She held on to his words when he took her to bed and made tender, passionate love to her. For the moment, he wanted to be with her, and that was enough. Miracles took a while, as he'd said, and she was so used to living for the moment with Bruno that she'd forgotten how to fear the future.

Or had learnt how to ignore its hovering menace.

He took her sightseeing in Funchal the next day, walking beneath the avenues of jacaranda and flame trees, their branches festooned with thousands of coloured light bulbs for the forthcoming carnival celebrations. With bulging carrier bags propped up against Ellen's feet, they relaxed in a café by the cathedral. Addan had insisted on buying some samples of the exquisite embroidery for her: tablecloths, napkins, linen.

'For momentoes,' he'd said, and her heart had sunk to her boots at the prospect of ever leaving him, and Madeira, before she'd resolutely put it from her mind.

She glanced at the chair beside her, smiling at the huge bouquet of flowers which he'd bought from the costumed flower-sellers, discussing with them which flowers were to be included. She'd wanted to kiss away his faint frown of concentration as he'd surveyed and approved various blooms, inhaled perfumes, chosen and discarded with such solemn sincerity.

Into the buttonhole of her navy and white striped jacket he'd tucked a single white freesia, savouring its fragrance as he did so. And her heart had bucked so fiercely as she'd looked at his bent head that she'd staggered in his light grasp and he'd steadied her with a cruelly gentle concern.

And now, basking in the early spring sunshine, he was lifting his face to the sun and she was incapable of keeping the love from her face, however vulnerable that made her.

'Heaven,' he murmured, his hand clasping hers. 'This is a wonderful break from work. You're wonderful to be with, Ellen.'

'Oh!' Joy filled her face. 'I am?'

'What a capacity you have for happiness!' he observed softly. 'For making the best of things.'

'It's the only way to survive,' she answered quietly. But her pulses were racing. Addan had warned her that their relationship could be short and sweet. Yet all her instincts told her it could be more lasting, given the right conditions. He had the ability to love, she was sure of that — after all, he'd had such feelings for that married woman, Maria.

She sobered. Addan was a hard man. Hard on himself; for the sake of honour, he'd ruthlessly suppressed his love. It gave her hope, though. Tough as he was, passion lay close beneath the surface. She felt sure she could touch his emotions. Perhaps she might even win his love.

Lifting her coffee-cup to her lips, she smiled secretly to herself and glanced over in case he'd seen her air of decision. Her smile broadened. His soft, dark eyes were centred longingly on a crocodile of tiny children, all in fancy dress.

'Oh, Addan!' she cried with delight, her hand resting on his arm. 'Aren't they sweet? I must get a photo.'

Laughing, she ran out, camera clicking at the moustached cowboy, the clowns, a minute Zorro and a handful of pirates. A four-year-old princess spread her skirts smugly for her, and she captured the moment with glee.

'*Obrigada!*' said Ellen, bobbing a little curtsy of thanks to the princess, whose enormous brown eyes were fringed by impossibly long lashes. A little boy, handsome even at that tender age as a Spanish matador, caught hold of the princess's hand and the little girl gazed up at him adoringly.

'He's mastered the strut and the swagger,' murmured Addan, coming to crouch beside her.

'Heartbreaker at the age of five!' she sighed. 'That arrogant stride. . .remind you of anyone?' She laughed wickedly.

He lifted her up, tweaked her nose and coaxed her to go for a swim with him in the Savoy Hotel pool, beside the glittering blue sea. They lazed in the warm sunshine afterwards, while he told her about his magical child-hood on the island.

Listening to his reminiscences, she knew for certain that he must have the Quinta if they parted. Or even before. It rightly belonged to him — though, she sighed to herself, not yet.

Selfishly, perhaps unfairly, she knew her possession of the Quinta kept him with her. At this fragile moment in their relationship, it was possible he might tire of her before she could prove she wasn't as awful as she'd been painted. So wisdom overruled her generous heart.

But she would one day give it to him willingly. Much as she'd like to live at the Quinta forever, it was no longer her only asset. Addan's sense of honour had ensured that she had the sisal business and a little more security behind her.

The next day was blissful. Ellen and Thereza energetically black-leaded the old iron range, their hair tied up in scarves, their faces streaked with black.

'I remember Don Addan doing this,' reminisced Thereza.

'*Addan*!' giggled Ellen in amazement.

'He came back from the Seychelles very bad temper, when Bruno marry you.'

Ellen noticed Thereza didn't give Bruno the courtesy title of 'Don'. 'And cleaned the stove?'

'He was very angry. Impossible for days. I say to him,' said Thereza, waving the blackened toothbrush in the air vigorously, 'go do some hard work. So he cleans the stove.'

'I'd love to see him join in and help us now,' laughed Ellen, looking through the kitchen window. He was talking to a team of pruners in a friendly way. They didn't seem overawed by him. Respectful, perhaps — but he seemed courteous towards them too, as if he valued their skills. 'Is he a good man, would you say?' she asked idly.

Thereza straightened in astonishment. 'Good? He is a saint!' she cried.

'A saint?' exclaimed Ellen, open-mouthed.

'True. We all cry when he go, we laugh when he come back. You see. We have party at Rui's. He has girls —— ' She caught Ellen's sudden start and giggled. 'No! He is a good man. The girls are poor. . . I do not know the word. . . He gives money to keep them and mothers, fathers, brothers.'

'Charity?' suggested Ellen, fascinated. She worked on an intricate section of the stove, splattering black all over her face and not noticing it at all. 'He supports poor families?'

'In the village, this is so. Property and land is expensive. When parents die, all is divided so the children have small part of house, small part of land. Don Addan, he help people buy land to make a life.'

'Does the vineyard employ a lot of people?' Ellen was revising her opinion of Addan again. He was like a benevolent godfather, she thought in astonishment.

'Many. I do not know how many.' Thereza hesitated. 'Little Bruno, he nice boy. But — forgive me — he think of himself. The village very poor when Bruno own vineyard. Addan take care of everyone.' Thereza looked at her watch. 'Ellen, I must go, wash, help at Rui's. We see you one o'clock.'

'I can't wait!' she grinned, longing to see Addan's 'girls'. She'd never let him live this down!

Half an hour later she'd finished and was sipping a welcome coffee, watching Addan making telephone calls in the garden. He was working very hard, despite his air of being relaxed. She enjoyed looking at him. His easy balance of authority and charm impressed her as he discussed business with his Brazilian directors.

'So you're Ellen.'

Happily she turned, frowned, and hastily rearranged her face in a smile of welcome. It was the infamous Maria, Addan's married blonde! 'Yes, I am. Hello,' she said, extending her hand.

'I am Maria de Almeida, a friend of Don Addan's.' The woman didn't sound very pleased to see her either.

'Can I get you some coffee?' asked Ellen politely.

'Black. No sugar.' Maria sat at the table and fastened her eyes hungrily on the lazily lounging Addan, his face animated as he discussed some deal.

'I'll tell him you're here,' said Ellen wryly.

'No.' Maria's contemptuous gaze swept over Ellen's filthy face, the concealing scarf on her head and the grubby clothes. 'Working for your keep, are you?' she drawled

In the act of placing the cup in front of the woman, Ellen stopped in surprise, and then laughed. 'I look a sight, don't I?' she said ruefully, comparing herself with the woman's immaculate dark beauty. Everything scrubbed, clean, groomed, she thought. Whereas she. . .! 'I fancied helping do the stove. It's been rather fun. Would you like to join me?' she asked mischievously.

'Certainly not! I don't do manual work.' Maria picked up the cup and headed for the garden doors, then turned gracefully. 'I hope you know what a dreadful reputation you have around here,' she said coldly. 'We read about your wedding. It sounded awful.'

'It was rather,' said Ellen disconcertingly.

There was a low chuckle and she saw that Addan had appeared at an open side-window. 'Morning, Maria. Sizing up the opposition?'

'I—my goodness, Addan!' said Maria with disdain. 'I really don't see your grubby little sister-in-law as any opposition. Now you are naughty, not telling us you'd arrived in Madeira after all this time,' she scolded pertly. 'I came to ask you to dinner tonight——'

'I was taking Ellen to see the Carnival,' said Addan lazily. 'But we'll come to dinner if it's well before that.'

'I wasn't asking her,' said Maria rudely.

'We come together or not at all,' smiled Addan.

'Does she have any decent clothes?'

Ellen's mouth opened at the insult. Her aggrieved eyes met Addan's and mellowed at the amusement on his face as he watched the by-play between the two women. 'I could wear something of Thereza's,' she suggested, wide-eyed.

'It'll have to do, won't it?' said Addan, deadpan.

Maria smirked. 'If you want to bring her, I suppose you must. Seven. On the yacht—you know which berth.' Her voice lowered huskily. 'You've been there often enough, darling. Must fly, lots to do. Bye, darling.'

'You don't have to take me,' said Ellen in a low voice when Maria had gone. 'Go on your own if you want to.'

'I want to show you off,' grinned Addan.

'I'm not your newest toy or acquisition.'

'Wash you face and hands and come outside,' he said easily. 'Thereza's child has arrived. Keep an eye on her while I make a few more calls, will you?'

'Oh, I'd love to!' she cried, putting away her apprehension about a dinner—however brief—with the scornful Maria. Yet, she thought, a glint in her eyes, perhaps Maria might get something of a surprise that evening when Cinders turned out to be wearing a St Laurent creation and dead set on charming the Prince.

'You take one of these,' Addan was saying in Portuguese to a small girl outside. He picked one of the orange flowers from the climber on the wall. 'And rub the bottom of the trumpet, see? On your forehead.' Ellen paused, her heart lurching. He was charming and never more so than with this child. 'Then you put it to your lips, and. . .'

The child—and Ellen—burst into delighted laughter at the thin trumpet sound that emerged from the flower.

'Let me!' cried the child.

'And me!' Ellen ran forward and picked a flower.

'This is Manuela,' said Addan fondly. He leaned forward encouragingly and the little girl blew. Her face was a picture when she managed eventually to make a sound from the flower trumpet and Addan was able to leave her, with some reluctance, she noticed, in Ellen's hands.

Little Manuela stole Ellen's heart at once. She took the child on to her lap in the big linen hammock strung between two magnolias, and listened to her solemn childish voice reading a fairy tale as she practised her English.

As a reward, Ellen brought her an iced drink and some Carnival biscuits and they curled up in the hammock again, listening to the soft splash of the fountain and the rustle of the papyrus grass nearby. Somehow, Ellen found herself reading from the book and the little girl's eyes became rounder and rounder at the story of Sleeping Beauty.

'I'll finish the story,' came Addan's quiet voice. 'You need to change for lunch. Something casual.'

She looked up and shaded her eyes, smiling at the tenderness of his expression. 'I can read, you see,' she said. 'When I'm relaxed.'

'So I heard. Bruno said you couldn't. I wish I could make you out,' he husked, lifting Manuela into his arms and giving her a hug. The little girl kissed him warmly and his attention was diverted to throwing the happily squealing child up in the air and catching her.

Ellen thought of the twin excitements of fear and relief and smiled again. 'It's no mystery why I can read today. I have dyslexia,' she said, as he settled Manuela, ready to continue the story. 'When I'm under stress, I have problems and the letters become a leaping jumble. I'm happy today; happier every minute that passes.'

'I'm very glad,' he said softly.

Her sweet smile lit her face — and turned to mischief in an instant, as she remembered. 'By the way, Thereza's told me you have a harem,' she said, setting off to the house and calling back over her shoulder. 'I'm longing to compare notes!'

His amiable grin remained in her mind while she showered and slipped on a fresh cotton skirt and top in a cerulean blue that matched her eyes and the Madeiran sea. And, when she popped her head out of the window, his dark head was bent over the child, a loving arm around her, and she felt all the love swell up in her heart and flow out to him.

Addan was, perhaps, she mused, a good man to those he loved and trusted. A saint. If only she could be sure.

The bar was hopping with people, all jammed in one small room decorated with streamers and balloons for the Carnival. Everyone knew and had affection for Addan, it seemed, and she was quite bewildered at the number of gorgeous young teenage girls, all dressed in short frou-frou gold lamé skirts and ruffled bodices, with enormous frilly pancake hats in brilliant scarlet.

'Costumes,' he said, seeing Ellen's amazed expression. 'They're in the same troupe for the Carnival.'

'I'm relieved,' she giggled. 'I wondered for a moment if I'd have to wear one as part of my harem uniform.'

His arm swept around her waist. 'You're the only one I want in my harem,' he murmured and she blushed, to the roar of amusement from everyone around them. The girls began to tease Addan and, to her astonishment, he too coloured faintly and seemed bashful.

'Women!' he grumbled happily. 'Come and see the oven.'

'Not another one for me to clean!' she wailed in mock-horror.

'No!' Laughing, taking a long time to weave his way through the friendly back-slappings and greetings, Addan took her to the kitchen where great iron skewers were being thrust into a large furnace.

'What's the gorgeous perfume?' she asked.

'Laurel leaves. This is *espetada*,' he said, abandoning her and helping Rui's wife to load the finished kebabs on to a stand. 'Beef on a skewer. This is ours. Let's take it outside and get out of everyone's way.'

They ate lunch on a terrace overlooking the misty Desertas Islands, amid a babble of chatter, each long table decorated with nasturtiums—wounds of God, Thereza called them. The girls energetically showed everyone their routine for the Carnival, and Ellen looked around her feeling so dizzy with happiness that she thought she'd never stop smiling.

'I think we must leave,' Addan said to Rui, at four o'clock that afternoon. 'We have some things to do before we go out tonight.'

'What things?' asked Ellen.

Addan's sidelong glance made her go bright red in confusion and she allowed him to sweep her away after a general swamping of hugs and kisses from everyone there.

'You embarrassed me,' she whispered as they walked back to the Quinta.

'I'm sorry, my darling,' he said lovingly. 'I thought you'd taken on board all those hints and glances I was giving in your direction.' He drew her close to him. 'You were wonderful with my friends. That was one of the best times I've ever known and I wanted to bring you home and make love to you in the garden before the sun sets.'

'Oh, Addan!' she said, her eyes starry.

He buried his head in her hair. 'We don't have long——'

'Almost three hours!' she laughed.

'Of course. Three hours.' He was silent for a moment and a little withdrawn. Then he hugged her as if he never wanted to let her go.

Sweetly, tenderly, they explored pleasure with one another beneath the spreading trees. Ellen felt a sense of deep fulfilment. She was sure he loved her. No man could look at a woman as Addan looked at her and not be in love. But when would he admit it? she wondered.

'That is not one of the maid's dresses.' Maria's eyes narrowed as she surveyed the shimmering black sheath.

'I managed to find one of my own,' smiled Ellen, finding Maria's black anger rather sad.

'I forgot you were a rich widow,' said Maria coldly.

'This is a beautiful boat,' said Ellen, feeling sorry for the woman. 'How lucky you are!'

'You're late, darling,' said Maria, deciding to pay attention to Addan alone. 'We're about to start.'

'It took longer getting Ellen dressed than I thought,' he said suavely.

There was pain in Maria's eyes and Ellen felt upset. Addan was being cruel. 'You saw how dreadful I looked earlier,' she said easily. 'I needed time for my transformation scene,' she giggled, with a friendly smile.

'Slut!'

Ellen reeled in horror at the venemous word and felt Addan's hand tighten in hers.

'Apologise,' he said quietly and she saw his face was white with rage.

'Please,' said Ellen huskily. 'Maria has heard rumours about me and it's no wonder she's not too keen to have me here on her yacht and to eat at her table. The rumours were lies and I'm not a slut,' she said to Maria. 'And I hope you'll accept me as you'd accept any of Addan's relatives. Shall we go below before your dinner is spoiled?'

Maria lifted her head proudly, but there was faint admiration in her eyes. 'Very well. We go below. You, Addan, will sit by me.'

'Thank you,' he said with icy courtesy. 'But I want Ellen near me. And no unpleasant remarks. Understand?'

In the opulent cabin of the sleek yacht, she sat quietly, bathed in dreams from the pleasure of the day—and sleepy from Addan's lovemaking. Her eyes flicked up now and then from the endless meal to admire Addan sitting opposite. Their legs entwined and he smiled at her, raising his glass in a silent toast.

'He loves you.'

Her head jerked to Maria's husband, sitting next to her. 'I beg your pardon?' she asked, a little flustered.

The man smiled wistfully. 'You look at each other

with such love. Ah, I envy you. Maria and I have known him since we were children. Don't let him go. He is a good man and he loves you.'

'I don't —— ' she began uncertainly.

'Ellen!' called Addan, smiling at her. 'Don't let that old rogue flirt with you! He's a taster, a *provador*, and they're dangerous men!'

She was aware of Maria's livid face at Addan's affectionately teasing jealousy. 'Surely not more dangerous than you?' she asked softly, unable to hide her love.

There was a hush around the table. Everyone's eyes were on them. 'I do hope not. Have a strawberry.' He held it out in front of her mouth and she opened her lips to protest. But he tipped her chin with one forefinger and tucked the sweet, ripe fruit between her teeth with a sensual gesture that left her bereft of air in her lungs.

'Please!' scathed Maria. 'I'd be glad if you didn't flirt at my table, Ellen.'

'She's blameless. It was my fault,' Addan confessed, his eyes still on Ellen's troubled blue ones. 'I'm sorry, Maria. I apologise, everyone. I can't —— ' He shrugged helplessly. 'Who could resist her? I'm. . .bewitched.'

People laughed indulgently. 'The day a man can't look at a woman with such love, Addan,' said Maria's husband, 'I for one will stop eating.'

Ellen went pink but found herself laughing with the others. The man had shown an appreciation for his food during the meal and was obviously known as a gargantuan eater.

'Are you staying long?' a woman asked her.

'It's difficult to say,' she answered guardedly.

'Well, you must get Addan to take you on the Monte toboggan run,' the woman said.

'I've heard of it,' said Ellen eagerly. 'The wicker basket on runners. Addan, can we go?'

'Anything you want,' he said lovingly and there was a ripple of laughter. 'I suggest you watch first. Ellen's a bit scared of heights,' he told the guests. 'It's quite a dramatic run—rather like a big dipper. Ernest Hemingway said it was the strongest emotion in his life.' Addan's mouth quirked. 'But then, Hemingway had never met you, had he?'

'Oh!' she breathed, stunned by his public compliment.

'I'll show you my island,' Addan continued huskily, reaching out for her hand, oblivious, it seemed, to everyone there. 'We'll go to the mountains, we'll visit the north coast and drive beneath sheeting waterfalls. I'll show you Risco, Camacha, Ribiero Frio, Levada do Norte. . .'

She smiled, squeezing his hand, her eyes awash with love. The words sounded like music when he spoke them. 'Thank you,' she said simply, realising what he was doing. He was making sure that everyone knew that she, Ellen, was very important to him and, whatever the rumours, she was to be accepted by them.

'My pleasure. Now,' he said, rising from his seat, 'if everyone will excuse us, I know you've all seen the Carnival dozens of times, but Ellen hasn't. Thank you for the meal, Maria, Luis,' he said with a little bow. 'It was exquisite as always.' He reached over and kissed Maria's hand very correctly while Ellen said her goodbyes to everyone else and then received a chilly farewell from Maria herself.

'I'll lift you down,' he said to Ellen, leaping lightly from the yacht on to the pontoon. For a few moments he held her in his arms.

'Shouldn't we hurry?' she murmured into his hovering mouth. 'The Carnival?' She was answered with a long, endless kiss. 'I love you,' she sighed.

'I could ask for nothing more. Now let's have fun,' he murmured. 'Come on!' Laughing, he began to pull her along and they hurried with the streaming crowds to where the procession was to set off.

Cuddled up to him, she watched the themed floats with their gorgeous costumes and enthusiastic bands go by, waving madly when his 'girls' went by in a vibrant

whirl of colour and a sexy samba rhythm. When the last
float passed, its young men in starred tunics dancing
energetically to a space-age band, they raced like
gleeful children behind the cheering crowds all the way
down the hill to the centre of town, where they watched
it all over again.

'Enjoy it?' he murmured, on the way back in the car.

Ellen stretched languorously. 'Mmm,' she said,
untangling streamers from her hair and fixing them so
they trailed out of the window. 'You do know how to
have the kind of fun I like.' She leaned back.

He chuckled. 'I liked the spectacle of you with your
skirts hitched up to your knees, racing like the wind
down the Avenida! I felt like a young man again. For
too long I've felt old.' He let his hand caress the nape of
her neck. 'I have the awful feeling that Bruno lied about
you,' he added softly. 'I believe you did hate the life he
led. You've behaved quite differently from how I
expected, fitting in with Thereza, the villagers, my
friends——'

'Not Maria, I'm afraid,' she said quietly.

'Maria is a foolish woman,' he said in a hard tone.
'She has a husband who adores her and who is the best
taster on the island in my opinion, and gives her a
wonderful life. They were in love once but she's become
hard and grasping. I'm afraid she is one of those women
who want all men to be a little in love with her.'

'As you were once,' she reminded him feeling a stab
of jealousy.

He made no reply and clammed up. Ellen had to be
content with the fact that he'd publicly declared that his
interest now lay elsewhere. But, when he made love to
her that night on the soft rugs in the drawing-room, she
felt a sadness that her days with him might be num-
bered too.

# CHAPTER NINE

THEY returned to the Savoy the following evening to see a folk-group. Excited at the prospect, Ellen had dressed up in a scarlet bootlace-strapped sheath with an impossibly short skirt and an overlay of stiff, rustling taffeta.

'You look. . .fabulous!' he breathed, his sharp intake of breath and his eyes telling her so long before he spoke.

Ecstatic, she tipped up her head, making the huge diamond earrings swing crazily. 'I feel it!' she cried happily. 'And you are a wow! Do a strut for me,' she demanded, wickedly teasing.

'New tux,' he explained drily. 'My tailor in Rio is always imagining my muscles are expanding.

'I expect he needs the business,' she said kindly, intentionally deflating his ego a little.

'He gets plenty from me. Do I do you justice?'

'I seem to have broken the rule that says never to go out with a man more devastating than you,' she sighed. He said nothing, just gazed at her and she sensed a deep affection in the warmth of his eyes. 'Oh, Addan!' she cried in delight, twirling around the hallway, too exuberant to stay still. 'I can't remember when I've been deliriously happy!'

'Oh, I'm sure you can,' he said in amusement. 'Didn't I satisfy you last night?'

'Endlessly,' she grinned, rolling her eyes. 'Anyway, I'm looking forward to enjoying this evening.'

'One of us might as well,' he said laconically.

There was a silence. 'Is there something wrong?'

'Should there be?' he countered, his eyes hooded.

'All at once you're different.' She felt a spasm of fear. 'Are you tired of me?' she whispered.

'No. Far from it. Don't take any notice of me. I'm merely protecting myself,' he said lazily, his eyes alarmingly secretive.

'What on earth from?' she asked in amazement.

'You. I really don't want to get swept into your spell, you see. You're too enticing by half. There are invisible sparks shooting out in all directions from you and all I want to do is take you, here, now, and to hell with the folk evening and spoiling your make-up and that incredibly saucy dress.' His mouth curved into a sensual arch that sent ripples through Ellen's veins.

'I'm glad you want me,' she said honestly and felt encouraged by the twitch of his mouth. He found her dangerous! That was promising. 'I'm longing to see the folk-dancing!' she cried excitedly. 'Please let's go!'

'Tuck those legs well away from my sight,' he advised in a hungry growl, his eyes flickering up and down her black-stockinged thighs. 'And behave demurely — if you know how.'

They danced to begin with, to a wild jazz band, the music getting faster and faster, the crowds on the enormous dance-floor whirling and laughing around them. Gradually Addan's strange mood eased and in his arms she felt utterly complete and content.

'We'll never get out of this!' he chuckled, as yet another flurry of curling streamers cascaded over them, entangling them in pinks and yellows and blues.

'I don't care,' she said dreamily.

He held her closer, swaying with the exotic, erotic music. 'I could dance with you forever, you're so. . . compatible with me.' His mouth nibbled her ear. 'Identical rhythms in our bodies. Perfect fit.' Addan's firm hand on her spine pressed a little harder so that she could feel her curves melding into his body.

'You know,' she mused, lifting her arms around his neck and looking at him with serious eyes, 'people here know how to have a good time. I always hated. . .' Her voice died away and then she gave a half-laugh, seeing his questioning eyes. 'No. That's telling tales out of school,' she said.

'Say it. Tell me,' he said quietly.

'It — it was the people we went around with,' she said in a low tone. 'They always looked bored and pretended to look down their noses at simple, ordinary pleasures.'

'Like dancing cheek to cheek?' he murmured.

'Mmm,' she sighed, as they did just that. 'It's so much nicer here, where people aren't pretending to be sophisticated and blasé. I feel very much at my ease here with you. I'd be happy to stay forever,' she said softly.

He stiffened. She looked up in alarm, but he'd been swung out of her arms by a group of people forming a conga. Darting up to him, she saw that his face wore a half-smile. Relieved, she wriggled into the conga and he placed his hands on her small waist, so that she was intensely conscious of him close behind her while the line of dancing revellers quartered the huge ballroom.

Exhausted, laughing, the rhythm drumming into her mind and body, she surrendered herself to the moment till the beat changed and the lead singer began to croon a soft *fado*, sweet, gentle, caressing the words in a lush, slow sibilance.

Addan held her glued to his body, her head pressed against his chest, and she was in a haze that had nothing to do with drink, only the intoxicating oblivion that being close to him brought. Flipping her drowsy eyes open, she felt her heart miss a beat. He was looking down with an intense tenderness and she could have been forgiven for thinking they were the eyes of a man in love. He smiled warmly and she snuggled up closer. Paradise was in his arms, she thought sentimentally.

The lights in the ballroom dimmed; the balloons and streamers, the yards of huge silk banners and the giant silver masks became barely discernible.

Addan's fingers threaded through her hair time and time again as if he found its silky strands irresistible to touch. 'Tell me your secrets,' he murmured. 'How you enchant men ——'

'There's only one man I want to enchant and that's you,' she said simply.

His arms tightened around her. 'I have an in-built resistance to taking that final, fatal bite of Eve's apple,' he said huskily.

'Don't you want love, children, happiness?' she asked huskily.

'In theory,' he agreed laconically, his lips brushing her temple. 'How do I ever know a woman loves me and not the size of my wallet?'

'You'll know,' Ellen said with quiet passion. 'You'll know the way your heart jumps when she looks at you, how you can't stop touching her. . .' She smiled. Addan had hastily stopped nuzzling her neck. Her shimmering eyes held his and she spoke so softly from choking emotion that he was forced to bend his big head to her. And he couldn't resist rubbing his cheek against hers. Again she smiled, hope swelling inside her. 'You'll know,' she continued, 'when you want to be with her even doing the most ordinary things. Like shopping. Or walking. And. . .when you can't imagine the future without her.'

'I hope you didn't get that from a magazine, Ellen,' he whispered into her hair. 'I'd like to think that was from the heart.'

'Of course it is,' she said shakily. 'That's how I love you.'

'You're very disconcerting,' he frowned.

'I'm honest.'

'And does that mean you've told me everything there is to know?' he enquired. 'All your secrets?'

'Secrets are two-way,' she answered huskily, her hand marvelling at the heavy beating of his heart.

'This is the moment to take risks, if ever there was one,' he murmured. 'When we seem to be closer than at any other time.'

'You're right. I don't like having secrets from you,' she confessed. 'I'll tell you. . .part of one.' She paused, planning how to keep faith with Bruno and yet reveal some of the truth to Addan. 'I dread angering you.' His eyebrow lifted in surprise and his hands, which had been wandering along her spine, suddenly stilled. 'Not because I'm afraid of you!' she said quickly. Because, she thought sadly, it could end their relationship.

'You should be afraid,' he growled, his lips brushing her forehead with a delicate sensuality. 'I could hurt you badly.'

'Yes. You could,' she admitted. And very soon, perhaps, she thought, her hands going clammy.

'Your frankness is disarming.'

'I have to tell you — if I don't, I'll feel like I'm holding something back that's important. You won't like what I'm going to say, though,' she told him hoarsely, her voice shaking with nerves.

Two black eyes glittered down on her. 'Then we should sit down somewhere private,' he said softly. Looking rather cold and daunting, he led her to the far corner of the room, away from everyone else, and in the darkness he pushed her against the wall and placed his hands on either side of her so that she was a virtual prisoner. 'Tell me,' he demanded, menacingly quiet.

She hung her head. Some day he would have needed to know. How sad that it should be tonight, when she'd been so happy! 'It's about — about the companies Bruno inherited,' she mumbled.

'The Torre inheritance.'

'The inheritance. Oh, God!' she moaned.

'Get on with it, Ellen,' he muttered.

Ellen flicked a petrified glance up at him and wished she hadn't. He towered over her, hostile and forbidding, as if he might explode with temper any moment. 'Bruno's businesses — '

'Were built up over generations, with love, care, dedicated hard work, for the Torre children to inherit,' he said softly.

'I know that. Don't make it worse!' she groaned in distress. 'Oh, Addan! I knew at the time how awful it was! You don't know. . .' She caught the dangerous tightening of his mouth and blurted out the terrible truth. 'You'll never forgive me! I sold them!' she said hoarsely.

Addan inhaled and exhaled, his face like stone. Her terror-ridden eyes were locked to his as she waited in awful anticipation for his reaction, bracing herself for whatever he might throw at her.

'You've taken a long time to admit that,' Addan said unemotionally.

Her eyes widened. 'You don't sound very surprised!'

He shrugged. 'I'm not. I knew.'

'*What*?' she gasped. 'You never said. . .' Ellen gulped, afraid of the ice-cold set of his face. 'All this time, you knew?'

'All this time. I knew that the minute he was dead you turned all his assets into cash. The yacht, the apartments, the villas, the antiques, the businesses. I've been waiting for you to tell me.'

'You should have said ——'

'Would it have made any difference?'

She looked at him helplessly. 'It might have helped me to understand your hostility. But you've obviously come to terms with what I did. We—you didn't mind us——'

'Sex has nothing to do with this,' he growled.

'*Sex*?' she gasped. 'It wasn't just that, Addan, and you know it!'

'Keep your voice down,' he frowned.

'You are angry. Please understand; I couldn't help it, I had to sell,' she said miserably.

'Really? Would you like to explain why you had to sell my brother's inheritance for a mess of potage?' he asked in clipped, precise tones. His eyes blazed, revealing a little of the anger that smouldered beneath the tight control. 'So did Esau sell his birthright to Jacob; to acquire material comfort at the expense of something which had a real, lasting value. What was your problem, Ellen? Did you really need so much money for your old

age, when your body and your face were no longer your
fortune?'

She stared, appalled. 'That's unfair! We've been so
close. . .' She choked back a sob. 'After the things
we've done together, you can't believe I'm that shallow——'

'Then tell me why.'

'I can't! I'd betray Bruno. I promised. Trust me,
believe in me!' she pleaded. 'You have every right to be
angry but can't you work out a reason I might have
had?'

Please, she begged him silently. Release me from my
promise. Guess the reason and I'll have to confirm it.

'Other than greed? No,' he growled. 'You weren't
interested in boring old businesses, which needed nur-
turing and managing. You indicated as much when I
gave the Angolan sisal operation to you. The moment
Bruno was dead, you cold-bloodedly shed the work of
generations! All you were interested in was hard cash.
A considerable sum of money, wasn't it?' he hissed.

'A fortune,' she whispered, heartbroken. 'But——'

'No excuses! None exists! Now you understand why I
could never let down my guard with you. Despite
appearances to the contrary—and some charming little
ways—you're a mercenary female. You sold up
because you didn't give a damn about tradition and the
livelihood of others. You've thrown away my family's
inheritance.'

She lowered her head. Bruno threw it away, she
wanted to cry and she longed for Addan to know the
truth and to comfort her for all the pain she'd suffered.
'I'm sorry,' was all she could say. 'You must think badly
of me.'

'I do. It strengthens my position a little, though,' he
said softly. 'You feel guilty. You owe me a lot.'

'I can give you no more than what I'm giving you
now,' she said dully. 'You have my love. You have my
body.'

'I want more. And I'm going to get it.'

His unnerving threat was interrupted by the sound of clapping. Dimly Ellen heard music and bells and she turned to see what Addan was frowning at. 'The folk-dancers,' she said in despair. 'Please let's go! I couldn't bear to watch ——'

Addan scowled. 'You will stay. People will wonder what we're doing over here and I have a reputation to keep up even if you haven't.'

'No!' she cried, appalled at the idea.

Her arm was twisted behind her back and Addan thrust his furious face close to hers. 'You will do this for me!' he ordered tightly. 'We will stay for a time and then we will make a dignified exit.'

'Don't do this to me!' she whispered. 'Don't hate me!'

'Make a scene here,' he said menacingly, 'shame me as you've shamed the Torre name by your antics across Europe with your stupid jet-setting friends, and I'll create such a hell for you with some salacious Press stories—even at the expense of my own honour—that you'll wish you'd never pranced on Bruno's yacht intending to wind him around your little finger!'

Numb, upset by his rightful anger, Ellen had no choice but to let him walk her to her seat. Sullen-faced, she stared at the dancers, refusing to show interest. Men in white shirts and knee-length trousers danced happily around pretty girls in swirling striped skirts and little red capes. Lutes and scrapers accompanied the accordion and a girl with a sharp, clear voice sang of love and sorrow while Addan's hand stayed clamped to her shoulder in a travesty of affection.

'. . .mimicking the small steps of the slaves' chained ankles,' explained the glamorous woman describing the dances in several languages.

Ellen started, and slowly turned her head to the stony-faced Addan. 'Is that what you've been doing to me?' she asked bitterly. 'Binding me with chains and making me your slave?'

'Have I succeeded?' he asked quietly.

'Step by step,' she replied, her voice flat and lifeless. 'Take me back now.' To her horror, she saw that the dancers were among the tables now, encouraging the audience to rise and join a dancing circle in the middle of the room. Fun and games were something she could not cope with right now. 'Addan, we've sat here long enough! I want to leave!' she pleaded, pulling at his vice-like hand.

'You'll stay till I want you to go,' he said grimly. 'You'll do everything I want you to do. For too long, my brother was manipulated by you and now it's my intention to manipulate you.' He leaned close, his hot breath harsh on her face. 'I made a vow to my dead brother's memory,' he said softly. 'I'm keeping it.'

'I — oh, no — !'

He'd risen, swept her into the circle and then immediately abandoned her, two male dancers cheerfully grasping each of her trembling hands, whisking her on shaking, half-stumbling legs in a joyous dance. Or, at least, it was joyous for everyone else. She was in a total daze.

Across the other side of the floor was Addan, his dark eyes watching every move she made. With a tremendous effort, Ellen tried to clear her head and plan a dignified escape. She was running again, she thought miserably. And now she had nowhere to go.

Her huge eyes rested on the two young women on either side of Addan and narrowed at their open-mouthed admiration for him. She glared at them when they began to speak to him but they didn't notice. Flirting! she thought angrily. They were flirting with him!

Suddenly, she saw Addan drawn into the centre of the circle by a middle-aged matron, dance with her, then kneel on a scarf she'd laid on the ground. It seemed to be some kind of traditional dance. They kissed one another chastely and then Addan was left in the ring alone to seek a partner.

Outraged, she bristled when he smiled at the two

girls and moved towards them. Lacerating jealousy seared through her body, making her breath ragged with pain. Then he turned, his dark eyes clashing with her angry blue ones. And he came over, amused, dragging her reluctant figure into the centre of the ring, dancing with her as if no one else existed. With the triumph that he hadn't chosen either of the two girls came the despair that she cared so much.

'Tell me you love me,' he murmured, mesmerising her with his hypnotic eyes and wicked mouth.

Miserably she went through some kind of step with him. He forced her down to kneel on the scarf and almost thigh to thigh they swayed to the music, centimetres away from one another.

'Tell me,' he whispered. His mouth met hers with infinite sweetness.

She could crumble into dust or match his will-power, till one of them was the victor. Ellen, she told herself, you've been through hell and come out a survivor. You can come through this.

She'd stand her ground. Addan lifted her to her feet and handed her the scarf. Their eyes met and she saw pain, a bleak expression as if he'd wanted his suspicions of her to be confounded.

Somehow she'd do that. He was worth fighting for. If she loved him enough, she'd stay with this through thick and thin. And she offered up a silent prayer as she placed all her trust in the power of love.

'Of course I will. I love you,' she said from the bottom of her heart. 'I love you and I will go on loving you forever.'

The next few moments were a blur. Rough hands dragging her from the room, faces, stairs, the brilliantly lit foyer. And then they were driving, the smooth, prowling car hurtling along the mountain roads. He drove faster than she'd ever known anyone to drive on roads such as these, the tyres screeching when he forced the car around the blind corners with a skill that kept them tightly hugging the edge of the road.

If he lost concentration for one second, they'd crash into the mountain or go flying off the edge.

Bewildered, her body bruised where he'd flung her bodily into the car, Ellen clung, terrified, to her seat. Tears rolled unchecked down her cheeks but he ignored her, his face black as thunder, his eyes staring at the road and his body hunched and tense like a man possessed by the devil.

Somewhere high up in the mountains, with brilliant white snow gleaming against blood-red soil, he stopped and wound the window down, breathing out a hard, harsh breath as the icy night air filled the interior of the car. A cold-looking moon hung over the jagged peak in front of them. And Ellen let out a howl of misery that cracked across the stillness.

'So it hurts,' he growled.

'Hurts?' she yelled. 'Darn right it hurts! What do you expect? It's what you wanted, isn't it, to hurt me, to make me suffer? God, Addan! You don't even know that I've been hurt, over and over! You're breaking my heart! Don't you care?'

'Shut up!' he snarled, glaring at the innocent snow ahead. He took the keys from the ignition and jumped out. 'Wait here,' he ordered harshly. 'There's a rug in the back.'

'Where are you going?' she asked in alarm.

He stared down at her, his eyes glittering. 'Does it matter?' he asked viciously.

Ellen watched him stride across the snow into the darkness. He wore only a camel-hair coat over his dinner-jacket and black leather shoes. She opened the car door and was hit by an arctic blast of wind. 'Addan!' she yelled, afraid for him. 'Addan!' He was in a terrible temper. He might not even notice where he was going. . .'Oh, God!' she sobbed.

Wrapping the blanket around her shoulders, she began to plough through the crisp snow, her high heels hindering her badly, wrenching her ankles.

'Addan! Addan!' she yelled.

And when she saw him, relief rocketed through her freezing body. Then sheer terror. He was on the edge of a long, long drop, his strong, dark head uplifted, his profile sharp and proud against the snowy slope beyond.

'My darling Addan!' she whispered, her stomach wrenched with agonising fear.

Tremulously she forced herself to stay quiet, to walk softly, step by numbing step, wanting to scream with the icy pain. Then he turned slightly at the sound of her uncontrollably chattering teeth.

'For God's sake, Ellen, stay where you are!' he barked.

Her frightened eyes flicked to the black abyss to one side of her. 'No!' she shuddered, slowly walking towards him her face frozen with fear. 'Come back to the car,' she said hoarsely, trying to stay calm. 'I know you're upset, but——'

'Ellen,' he snapped. 'I told you to stay put——'

'I—was—afraid—for you!' she jerked, in a state of near-shock, the blackness closer, making her feel dizzy.

He frowned and pushed a tired hand through his hair. 'Afraid for *me*?' He let out a huge exhalation of breath which frosted in the night air. 'Don't move,' he told her curtly. 'I'm coming back.'

Not until he'd turned from the terrifying chasm did she let go. Her body slumped to the ground, drained of all strength. He was safe. Addan was safe.

There was something in the way he gathered her to him that comforted her. She was too exhausted emotionally to respond when he tried to make her open her eyes, so he assumed she had fainted. And the fact that he kissed her closed lids and groaned suggested that he felt something for her—even if, like her, he wished otherwise.

When he worked out why she'd sold up, she told herself, everything would be all right.

In the car, he rubbed her frozen hands and covered her face with warm kisses till she stirred. Then, without saying a word, he held her very close, roughly massaging her body so that the feeling returned to every tingling inch.

'Suicide is not my style,' he muttered into her ear. 'I just needed to get away from you.'

She winced. 'I can understand that. Where does that leave me?' she asked shakily.

'I still want you,' he said huskily, his eyes melting like black snow. 'I want you and I hate you.'

'Then it's unfinished,' she whispered. 'We have to finish this, one way or another.'

He held her effortlessly with his compelling stare, the electricity crackling between them. 'That's how I figured it,' he said softly. 'To the bitter end. "To the victor belong the spoils".'

'To love,' she replied with a quiet defiance.

He smiled and his mouth came down on hers brutally, driving all coldness from her body and all thoughts from her mind. 'How tough are you?' he whispered. 'Don't you ever crack?'

'Kiss me,' she said fiercely, trying not to let the despair show. 'Kiss me and don't stop.'

Cool fingers crawled up her thighs, snapping the suspenders. She moaned into Addan's mouth and he peeled off her stockings, caressing her thighs, the backs of her knees, her calves. He lifted her legs so that they were tucked around him and then lifted her bare foot to kiss the sole.

'Beautiful,' he said thickly.

Ellen closed her eyes. She could feel his mouth surrounding each toe, sucking deeply with an eroticism that was making her breath ragged. Her hands reached out to his tie. She loosened it then fumbled blindly with the buttons of the crisp shirt. All the while, Addan's mouth was stealing up the inside of her leg.

There was a tearing sound and she looked down at her ruined dress in shock. 'Not with anger!' she whispered, watching his hands take each edge of her bodice and open it up. Her breasts tumbled gladly into his hands, pale moons in the dim, silent interior.

'It's the only way,' he muttered. 'Pay your dues.'

Ellen groaned at the pain inside her. 'I want you to love me,' she said jerkily.

'Impossible.'

He lifted her on to his lap. Beneath his contemptuous, hungry eyes, she trembled. She leaned forward to kiss his throat tenderly, with all the feeling she could. A shudder ran through his body. 'Love me,' she said huskily.

'Damn you, Ellen!' he snarled. 'How can I? You did this to my brother! And look how callously you treated him!'

He flung her away and she was left to pull her dress together while he started the car and reversed violently back down to the turn-off. In silence they drove home. And Ellen vowed that she'd give him the Quinta the next day. It might show that she cared.

'Why?' was all he said, when she handed him the deeds and her letter surrendering the property to him.

'To show good faith.'

Across the expanse of mahogany desk, he seemed hollow-eyed as if he hadn't slept that night. Certainly he'd never come to bed, and she'd lain open-eyed and as cold as a mountain peak, wondering if she'd ever find his heart.

A pulse beat in his jaw. 'I accept. You're very clever. But not clever enough.'

His stillness, the ice-hard glitter in his eyes, daunted her. 'It's not meant to be clever,' she said quietly. 'I want you to have it, that's all.'

'Now I have everything,' he said expressionlessly.

'Not yet.' Her own eyes glittered with a despairing anger. 'You haven't got a heart.'

'I don't need one,' he said smoothly. 'Not when I have all my Brazilian businesses and all Bruno's mainland possessions. Including you.'

Ellen felt her spine stiffen. 'What did you say?' she asked.

'When you sold, I bought,' he said with careful clarity. 'Close your mouth, Ellen,' he drawled. 'I bought everything. I've had to pay the price, God knows I've had to pay the price!' he growled angrily. 'But the Torre inheritance is safely in my hands.'

Her hands found the top of the desk and she leant against it, shaking like a leaf. 'Oh, Addan! I'm so relieved!' she cried. 'That's absolutely wonderful! How —— ?'

'Don't!' he roared. He jumped up so violently that his chair overturned with a crash that made her gasp. 'Don't wriggle your way out of this by pretending to be pleased! You couldn't have given a toss about any of it, only that you were rich beyond your wildest dreams!' He leaned forward, menacingly. 'OK. I've got the Quinta. It's what I came for.'

She swayed in horror. 'What?' she whispered, sinking to a chair. 'You planned this?'

'I wanted my home,' he said grimly. 'I didn't care how I got it. I was prepared to lie, cheat, steal,' he said huskily, 'even sleep with a whore.'

'No!' She felt her throat close up, the retching sickness high in her throat.

'This is it, Ellen,' he snarled savagely. 'That moment when you think you're home and dry and then all your dreams are dashed by a terrible blow. This is the blow. And I am savouring it.'

'I can't believe. . .' He didn't love her. He never had. It had all been a sham, a pretence. First Bruno, then Addan. 'Ohh!' she cried hoarsely, the word wrenching from the very depths of her betrayed body.

'Thank you for giving me my home,' he said sardonically. 'Now leave. Time to say your goodbyes and get out of my sight. There's a plane in two hours. Be on it or I won't answer for the consequences. I'm quite prepared to concoct a story that will put you in gaol if necessary. You know that.'

'I — can't — move!' she breathed, her blue eyes enormous. But there was no compassion in his eyes. Nothing but a malevolent loathing. 'You said you wanted me — '

'I still do, God help me,' he snarled savagely, his teeth bared as if he wanted to tear her flesh apart. 'But there'll be other women. Less demanding.'

'Maria,' she said dully.

'No. I told you. When you saw her coming from the Quinta that first day you came here, she'd called — as she had for the last year — to check that Thereza was cleaning the place properly. She doesn't trust maids,' he said scathingly. 'Maria doesn't understand people like Thereza, that they do a job well because of their own self-respect.'

'Did you make love to Maria when she found you there?' croaked Ellen.

Addan's eyes blistered hers. 'No!' he snapped. 'I threw her out. Luis is my friend and I prize his work. I wouldn't jeopardise that for some quick tumble in the hay. What do you care, anyway?' he asked bitterly. 'There'll be a thousand women after you. Do you want me to write and tell you about each one?'

'No.'

Somehow the strength came to her, enough to stand proudly before him. 'I loved you, Addan, and you have deceived me as your brother did. I thought you might feel the same way in time. I was mistaken, as I was with Bruno. I'll go,' she said, her voice breaking up. 'I'll go!'

'Just one thing more.'

Her back to him now, she froze at the silky, venemous tone. 'More?' she whispered.

'Don't get too excited about the Angolan company I gave you. It's gone to the wall.' Ellen whirled, her face white with horror. 'Greed gets its own reward,' muttered Addan. 'I made sure that the company had every debt I could pile on it. And you, as its owner, are liable for every penny. Everything you own. The clothes on your back, the lipstick in your purse, the shoes on your feet.'

He smiled coldly but it seemed to hurt him to do so, all the lines of his face anguished. 'Every penny you made from selling Bruno's inheritance will have to be surrendered. You will have nothing. That, Ellen, is the extent of my vengeance.'

There was a long silence that grew in magnitude till the rustle of leaves outside was drowned in the thick wall of hatred between them.

Ellen began to laugh. Hysterical, she couldn't stop. 'You think you've stripped me of all my money?' she cried, weak from hysteria, the tears streaming down her cheeks. 'I have nothing!'

'I know ——'

'No, you don't!' she cried fiercely. '*I have no money*!' He looked blank. 'There was never any money to take.'

'But — you had a fortune ——'

'Goodbye, Addan,' she husked, broken-hearted.

He slammed against the door just as she reached it. 'Explain.'

'I can't. I promised. I keep promises. I have a sense of honour,' she said proudly.

'Bruno,' he growled. 'God, Ellen, you must tell me! I'll keep you here, I'll starve you if I have to, but tell me!'

'I won't! You wouldn't trust me. You didn't believe me ——'

'How could I?' he growled. 'Everything I'd heard about you warned me not to. It was Bruno, wasn't it?' Her lashes fluttered. 'Bruno. He was bad with money. . .mishandled it.' Ellen hardly breathed. 'You have to tell me,' he whispered.

'Give me one good reason why,' she said coldly.

'Oh, my God! Because I love you!'

Her eyes searched his. It was there: anguish, passion, a tearing longing. . .'I've been deceived before,' she said huskily.

Addan's head went back, an expression of agony on his face. 'Why do you think I kissed you in your cabin on that little boat in Amsterdam?' he said huskily. 'Why do you think Bruno was so determined to keep us apart?'

'But you said you were in love with a married woman, that you couldn't stay in Madeira because of her,' she frowned.

'You,' he said gently. 'It was you, all the time. I couldn't bear the thought of seeing you living with Bruno at the Quinta so I kept away. I loved you from the start. I told Bruno before you were even married how I felt about you. He said you weren't worth loving but I was obsessed and couldn't get you out of my mind. When I knew he meant to marry you, I followed you across Europe, trying to find you, to tell you what I felt about you, that I'd fallen for you at first sight, and the more you defied me and the more you spoke up for yourself and Bruno, the more I fell helplessly, headlong for you.'

The words had come out in a tumbling rush of harsh passion and they sounded completely sincere. 'Oh, no,' she whispered, quivering uncontrollably. She clutched at him and he seemed as tense as a bow-string.

'When I tracked you down in the Seychelles I could have killed Bruno, I was so angry,' he muttered. 'And then I felt guilty because I wondered then if you'd married him out of kindness because of his tumour——'

'Addan,' she said gently, 'you're forgetting. No one knew he had a brain tumour till six months before his death.'

He looked sadly into her eyes. 'He knew for years. I told him you should know and I thought you did. I suppose that's why he married you—to have some fun, to have the woman I wanted. It was his kind of revenge on life for dealing him a bad hand.'

'He lied.' She gave a sob. 'All those years with him! Nursing him, waiting on him hand and foot, never leaving his side, till I could hardly think or stand up. . . oh, Addan!'

'Now tell me,' he said hoarsely.

'Yes. It was Bruno who lost his own inheritance,' she

husked. 'He'd become a member of an insurance syndicate. That's why your revenge made me laugh. It was a bad time for insurance: bad risks, major disasters, hurricanes, oil spills, pollution claims. . .it meant substantial losses and Bruno had pledged his wealth so that even his cuff-links were called on.'

'You had to sell to pay what he owed,' said Addan quietly, his hands coming up to support her weary body.

'I went through a year of hell after he died,' she mumbled. 'All the paperwork was difficult for me. I struggled to understand everything but I was worried sick.'

'And all the time I was plotting my vengeance,' he said softly, taking her in his arms. 'I felt I'd let Bruno down. When I discovered you'd cashed in all your assets, I believed everything he'd said about you being vain and shallow and marrying him for his money. I told myself,' he sighed, stroking her hair gently, 'that you'd deliberately accelerated his death with drugs and drink and all-night parties.'

'I think he was very unhappy.' Ellen gave a shuddering sob. 'I was sorry for him and I did try to enjoy the parties he wanted and to love him, even though he never made lo. . .' She pressed her lips together quickly but Addan had already pushed her face up so that she was forced to look at him.

'Never what?' he frowned. 'Never *what*?' he grated ferociously.

'You came between us,' sobbed Ellen. 'He couldn't touch me! He said it was your fault. That's why he showered me with presents I didn't even want. You never even realised no man has ever made love to me.'

'Oh, God!' he said in a huge outrush of breath. 'You poor darling.' He rocked her in his comforting arms. 'Poor Bruno; impotent because he knew I loved you and that my life was in ruins because of his selfishness.' He kissed Ellen's forehead. 'Did you say "no man", Ellen?' he asked softly. 'You were so experienced ——'

'It was instinctive,' she said, giving him a faint smile. 'Passion, ignorance, hunger. I followed you and you led me like in a beautiful dance.'

'I led you?' he said with a gentle, loving laugh. 'I'm not sure. A woman in love is a terrible danger to a man. Ellen, you've been through fire and hell ——'

'And water,' she laughed, her spirits lifting with hope.

'Marry me and I'll protect you and love you for the rest of my days,' he said. 'We'll live here in paradise and I'll teach you about wine ——'

'And I'll teach you about love,' she said, her eyes shining.

'I'm learning,' he grinned. 'There have been Madeiran-English alliances for six hundred years ——'

'I'm all for tradition,' she cried happily. 'But Rio ——'

'Rio runs so smoothly it's boring. I've trained my management team too well. And I've been very homesick. I feel like come-back wine.' He smiled fondly at her querying brows. 'You never heard the story of how they discovered the potential of Madeiran wine. Some barrels went back and forth across the equator, rolling around on board, being heated and cooled, and when they were opened up instead of vinegar they found ——'

'Ambrosia!' she grinned.

'Are you always going to be finishing my sentences?' he asked, kissing her nose.

'I'll try,' she said demurely.

Her mouth was stopped by his lips in a tender kiss. Ellen sank happily into his embrace. Yes, he loved her. Very, very much. How happy she was, she thought dreamily.

'I hope the rest of our lives together will be smooth and uneventful,' murmured Addan.

'No. Take me to the edge sometimes,' she whispered. 'Excite me, thrill me. . .'

There was a paradise, she thought, as his mouth moved tenderly over hers. It was on this floating

Garden of Eden, in the beautiful surroundings of the Quinta das Magnolias, but most of all, she smiled dreamily, paradise was in the arms of the man you loved.

# *Welcome to Europe*

**MADEIRA** — 'Pearl of the Atlantic'

'The floating garden. . .' 'Island of Eternal Spring-
time. . .' These are just two of the phrases that have
been used to describe the island of Madeira. This
colourful island boasts a spectacular landscape, with
panoramic gorges, valleys and plateaux, sheer cliffs and
impressive waterfalls. There are picturesque villages to
explore, or, if you want a relaxing holiday, the gentle
pace of life here makes Madeira the perfect choice for
you. If you're looking for a combination of tropical
luxury and European comfort, there's simply nowhere
better.

## THE ROMANTIC PAST

It is uncertain who first discovered Madeira, but legend
has it that it was an Englishman, **Sir Robert Machin**. He
is said to have fallen in love with a beautiful young
woman called Anne d'Arfet. Unfortunately Anne came
from a very wealthy family who did not approve of the
match, and tried to force Anne to marry a man she
didn't love. In order to be together, Machin and Anne
were forced to flee, and so in 1346 they escaped by
boat, heading for France. The couple were caught in a

terrible storm and swept southwards, until they finally reached Madeira. No sooner had they disembarked when their ship was swept away in another storm. Anne, exhausted and despairing, died in her lover's arms, and a few days later Machin himself, unable to live without his beloved Anne, died of a broken heart.

However, it is generally agreed that the discoverer of Madeira was **Zarco**, who arrived in 1420, and named the place he found 'Isla De Madeira', meaning 'island of woods'. No traces of an earlier settlement on the island have ever been found.

**Christopher Columbus** is said to have lived in Madeira for several years before setting off to discover America. Although this is still disputed, it is known that Columbus did marry a young Madeiran woman, the daughter of one of the most important men in Madeira. How a seaman of humble birth managed this is not certain — perhaps it was a case of true love overcoming all.

Unfortunately love didn't always conquer everything in Madeiran history. In the early nineteenth century Maria Clementina, said to be the most beautiful girl on the island, was persuaded by her parents to become a nun. A couple of years later Parliament ordered the doors of all religious houses to be thrown open. Maria was released and fell in love with a handsome Portuguese officer. Before they could marry, the King cancelled the laws Parliament had made and Maria was forced to part from her loved one and spend the rest of her life in the convent.

Some romantic Madeiran traditions are still practised today. On the 24th of June, the feast of **São João** takes place. Madeirans hoping to find love write a name on pieces of paper, which are then folded and put in a bowl of water. If one is open the next day it will show the name of the person's future spouse.

**THE ROMANTIC PRESENT** — pastimes for lovers. . .

If you're travelling to Madeira you'll almost certainly want to visit the capital, **Funchal**. It's a good place to explore on foot, especially as all the footpaths in its centre are attractively made with black and white stones set in mosaic patterns. There are many interesting buildings to see, but top of your list has to be the cathedral (*Sé*) which was built between 1493 and 1514, in the early Gothic style.

Afterwards, why not visit the market area? This is particularly lively at weekends, when farmers come to display their produce. Among the many stalls, you're bound to see fish stalls with *espadas* — black swordfish with razor-sharp teeth — a speciality of the island.

After the hustle and bustle of the market, what could be more relaxing than a romantic stroll through one of the parks or in the **Botanical Gardens**? Here you can admire tropical trees, shrubs and flowers such as orchids, hibiscus and bougainvillaea, which the island is famous for. A walk here is a real feast for the senses — you can enjoy the beautiful colours of the flowers and breathe in their wonderful aromas.

For the young at heart, why not enjoy a ride on one of the traditional forms of transport on Madeira — a **toboggan**? You travel a distance of about three miles, from Monte to the centre of Funchal, in a wide wicker basket. The toboggan drivers, dressed in white, run alongside the toboggan, pushing it and braking where necessary. It's an exhilarating experience!

And if all this activity has made you thirsty, why not enjoy a taste of luxury and visit one of the world's leading hotels? **Reid's Hotel** has been host to kings, queens, George Bernard Shaw and Winston Churchill, among others. You might not be able to afford to stay there, but enjoying a sedate afternoon tea on the terrace is the perfect way to relax during a hectic day's sightseeing.

One interesting feature of Madeira is its *levadas* — water channels which were built for transporting water from the north of the island to the south. All were built with paths alongside them, and most visitors to the island will want to go *levada* walking, a great way of experiencing some of the most beautiful scenery in Madeira. One of the most important *levadas* is the Levada dos Tornos, and, walking beside it, you might first see women standing by the footpath doing washing in their stone troughs, then pass camellia and lemon trees, and further on view a breathtaking waterfall.

Madeira is such a pretty island that it seems a shame to confine yourself to Funchal. One of the most visited places in Madeira is **Camâra de Lobos**, and it's not hard to understand why. Its name means 'Seals' Chamber', because it is where Zarco saw a number of seals when he first arrived in Madeira. It's a picturesque little fishing village, virtually unchanged by time, and a favourite spot of Winston Churchill's. A sight not to be missed is nearby **Cabo Girâo**, the world's second highest sea cliff, at about 1,800 feet. But be warned — you'll need a good head for heights.

You might be interested in visiting **Camacha**, the centre of the wickerwork industry, where you can watch the work in progress and buy the finished items — from baskets and chairs to elephants and giraffes! And if you want to visit a typical Madeiran village, try **Santana**, with its little cottages with painted gables and thatched roofs reaching almost to the ground. Even the public toilets here are disguised as a thatched cottage!

Finding a souvenir of your holiday shouldn't be too difficult — there are so many to choose from! For a memento which captures the very essence of Madeira, you could take home some **flowers**. Orchids travel well, are long-lasting, and can be specially packed. **Wickerwork** is another popular souvenir — you'll find it hard to resist buying some if you visit Camacha — or you might choose some Madeiran **embroidery**, which is famous throughout the world.

When you're eating out in Madeira, you'll probably want to try the excellent fish. One of the specialities of the island is *espada* — a black and apparently delicious fish. Tuna fish steak is another typical dish. For a change from fish, try delicious *carne di vinho e alhos* — meat marinated in a wine sauce with garlic and laurel or fennel. And for dessert, what about *bolo do mel*, Madeira cake made with honey, cinnamon, spices and nuts? If you're so busy sightseeing that you haven't got time to sit down and eat, you're bound to come across stalls selling *espetada* — skewered beef — on almost every street corner.

And before or after your meal you'll probably want to try some **Madeira wine**, which the island has been famous for for centuries. There are four main types: **Malmsey**, the sweetest; **Bual**, which is less sweet and very fragrant; **Verdelho**, which is medium, and **Sercial**, which should be drunk cold as an aperitif. You might also like to visit the **Madeira Wine Company Lodge** and enjoy a guided tour — and, best of all, a chance to try some of the different wines!

For the perfect end to a romantic day in Madeira you can watch one of the magnificent sunsets. If you're very lucky you might even see the strange 'green flash' which sometimes follows a Madeiran sunset. Standing with your loved one watching the changing colours of the sky and inhaling the aromatic scent of flowers is a memory which will stay in your mind forever.

## DID YOU KNOW THAT. . .?

* Madeira is thirty-six miles long, fourteen miles wide and is situated just north of the **Canary Islands**.

* the unit of currency is the **escudo**.

* the language spoken in Madeira is **Portuguese**.

* there are **112 species of plants** currently growing in Madeira.

* if you want to tell a Madeiran you love him, you say '*Amo-te*'.

## LOOK OUT FOR TWO TITLES EVERY MONTH IN OUR SERIES OF EUROPEAN ROMANCES:

**NO PROMISE OF LOVE:** Lilian Peake (Switzerland)
Love-affairs by the dozen, but wedded bliss? Not for wealthy Rolf Felder. So was his engagement to Abigail merely a matter of convenience?

**LOVE'S LABYRINTH:** Jessica Hart (Crete)
Lefteris Markakis was arrogant, but undeniably attractive. The trouble was, he clearly despised English girls — and Courtney had walked right into the middle of his vendetta!

**IN NAME ONLY:** Diana Hamilton (Spain)
Javier Canpuzano had no doubt that Cathy was a bad mother to little Johnny. What he *didn't* know was that Cathy wasn't the child's mother at all. . .

**MASTER OF DESTINY:** Sally Heywood (Corfu)
Shelley had never forgotten Christos and their idyllic summer in Corfu. Then love had turned to hate. . . But now she was back, and Christos wanted his revenge. . .

# NEW from...

**MILLS & BOON**

## HEARTS OF FIRE
### *by Miranda Lee*

*Welcome to a new and totally compelling family saga set in the glamorous world of opal dealing in Australia.*

Laden with dark secrets, forbidden desires and scandalous discoveries. HEARTS OF FIRE unfolds over a series of 6 books as beautiful, innocent Gemma Smith goes in search of a new life, and fate introduces her to Nathan Whitmore, the ruthless, talented and utterly controlled playwright, and acting head of Whitmore Opals.

*BUY ONE GET ONE FREE!*
As a special introductory offer you can buy
Book 1 - 'Seduction & Sacrifice' along with
Book 2 - 'Desire & Deception'
*for just £2.50*

**Available from April 1994**
**Price: £2.50**

*Available from W. H. Smith, John Menzies, Volume One, Forbuoys, Martins, Woolworths, Tesco, Asda, Safeway and other paperback stockists.*
*Also available from Mills & Boon Reader Service, FREEPOST, PO Box 236, Croydon, Surrey CR9 9EL. (UK Postage & Packing free)*

# IT'S NEVER TOO LATE FOR SWEET REVENGE...

Adrienne's glittering lifestyle was the perfect foil for her extraordinary talents. A modern princess, flitting from one exclusive gathering to another, no one knew her as The Shadow—the most notorious jewel thief of the decade.

Her spectacular plan to carry out the ultimate heist would even an old and bitter score. But she would need all her stealth and cunning to pull it off —Philip Chamberlain, Interpol's toughest cop knew all the moves and was catching up with her. His only mistake was to fall under Adrienne's seductive spell!

## WORLDWIDE

AVAILABLE NOW                    PRICE £3.50

*Available from W.H. Smith, John Menzies, Martins, Forbuoys, most supermarkets and other paperback stockists. Also available from Worldwide Reader Service, Freepost, PO Box 236, Thornton Road, Croydon, Surrey CR9 9EL. (UK Postage & Packing free)*

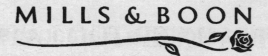

# MILLS & BOON

# Forthcoming Titles

## DUET
### Available in April

**The Betty Neels Duet**   **A SUITABLE MATCH**
**THE MOST MARVELLOUS SUMMER**

**The Emma Darcy Duet**   **PATTERN OF DECEIT**
**BRIDE OF DIAMONDS**

## FAVOURITES
### Available in April

**NOT WITHOUT LOVE** Roberta Leigh
**NIGHT OF ERROR** Kay Thorpe

## LOVE ON CALL
### Available in April

**VET IN A QUANDARY** Mary Bowring
**NO SHADOW OF DOUBT** Abigail Gordon
**PRIORITY CARE** Mary Hawkins
**TO LOVE AGAIN** Laura MacDonald

Available from W.H. Smith, John Menzies, Volume One, Forbuoys, Martins, Tesco, Asda, Safeway and other paperback stockists.

Also available from Mills & Boon Reader Service, Freepost, P.O. Box 236, Croydon, Surrey CR9 9EL.

Readers in South Africa - write to:
Book Services International Ltd, P.O. Box 41654, Craighall, Transvaal 2024.

# Next Month's Romances

Each month you can choose from a wide variety of romance with Mills & Boon. Below are the new titles to look out for next month, why not ask either Mills & Boon Reader Service or your Newsagent to reserve you a copy of the titles you want to buy – just tick the titles you would like and either post to Reader Service or take it to any Newsagent and ask them to order your books.

*Please save me the following titles:*     Please tick    ✓

| Title | Author | |
|-------|--------|--|
| AN UNSUITABLE WIFE | Lindsay Armstrong | |
| A VENGEFUL PASSION | Lynne Graham | |
| FRENCH LEAVE | Penny Jordan | |
| PASSIONATE SCANDAL | Michelle Reid | |
| LOVE'S PRISONER | Elizabeth Oldfield | |
| NO PROMISE OF LOVE | Lilian Peake | |
| DARK MIRROR | Daphne Clair | |
| ONE MAN, ONE LOVE | Natalie Fox | |
| LOVE'S LABYRINTH | Jessica Hart | |
| STRAW ON THE WIND | Elizabeth Power | |
| THE WINTER KING | Amanda Carpenter | |
| ADAM'S ANGEL | Lee Wilkinson | |
| RAINBOW ROUND THE MOON | Stephanie Wyatt | |
| DEAR ENEMY | Alison York | |
| LORD OF THE GLEN | Frances Lloyd | |
| OLD SCHOOL TIES | Leigh Michaels | |

If you would like to order these books in addition to your regular subscription from Mills & Boon Reader Service please send £1.90 per title to: Mills & Boon Reader Service, Freepost, P.O. Box 236, Croydon, Surrey, CR9 9EL, quote your Subscriber No:.................................... (If applicable) and complete the name and address details below. Alternatively, these books are available from many local Newsagents including W H Smith, J Menzies, Martins and other paperback stockists from 8 April 1994.

Name:................................................................................

Address:.............................................................................

.................................................Post Code:..........................

**To Retailer: If you would like to stock M&B books please contact your regular book/magazine wholesaler for details.**

You may be mailed with offers from other reputable companies as a result of this application.
If you would rather not take advantage of these opportunities please tick box ☐